IN WAY TOO DEEP

MONICA WALTERS

B. Love Publications

INTRODUCTION

Hello, Readers!

Thank you for purchasing and/or downloading this country hood love story. This story is book four of the Henderson's family novels. While it isn't necessary to read the others before this book, it will give you more insight into the characters in this story. The other three are Blindsided by Love (Storm), Ignite My Soul (Jasper), and Come and Get Me (Tiffany).

This work of art contains explicit language, child neglect and abuse, violence, and lewd sex scenes. This is also a redemption story. If any of the previously mentioned offend you or serve as triggers for unpleasant times, please do not read.

Also, please remember that your reality isn't everyone's reality. What may seem unrealistic to you could be very real for someone else. But also keep in mind that this is a fictional story.

If you are okay with the previously mentioned warnings, I hope that you enjoy the story Kenny and Keisha have been dying to tell. Please keep an open mind when reading and evolve as the characters do as well.

Monica

PROLOGUE

K enny

"I FUCKED UP IN THE WORST WAY AND HAVE BEEN FOR YEARS."

"Okay. So, in what way? That way we can start from the beginning."

"I've cheated for years and she finally had enough of my bullshit."

I was sitting here at a psychiatrist's office, trying to understand my actions. This shit was unforgiveable. Keisha was a damn good woman to me, and it was only so much she could take. All the fucking around was wrong on so many levels. My kids were suffering the most, though. I missed the hell out of them. After this last go 'round, Keisha left with my kids and moved back to her family in San Antonio, five hours away.

It had been two months since she'd left, and I felt like I was losing it. Depression was threatening to take me out, and the promise of seeing my kids on the weekends was all I seemed to be living for.

When they left, it was the first time I'd cried in a while. Every weekend, I flew my babies to town so we could have some time together. But Sunday through Thursday found me in my bedroom or at the convenience store. They always left on Sunday morning. But every weekend was about to come to an end. Keisha had said that it was wearing the kids out and it was my fault that I couldn't see them every day.

It *was* my fault and I couldn't argue with her. I was at her mercy. She could choose to keep my kids from me altogether. "So, how long were you with... I'm assuming your wife?"

"Yeah. We were married for almost twelve years and have two gorgeous kids. KJ is eleven and Karima is five."

"So, what were things like in the beginning? How did the two of you meet?"

Thinking back on that fateful, romantic day, really had me in my fucking feelings. I could feel the lump forming in my throat and my face was heating up. Pulling at my beard was a nervous habit that I had, and I realized I was doing that shit now. Bringing my hand to the couch I was sitting on, I began. "We met at a grocery store. I'd gone to San Antonio for a conference with my dad about something to do with the grass farms. I don't remember exactly. We were staying in a trailer as we often did. My brother, WJ, was cooking and ran out of seasoning. When I got to the store, it was pouring. It had been threatening to rain all day. As I grabbed the umbrella from the passenger seat, I saw this beautiful woman running to her car in the rain, with a basket full of groceries."

The therapist was watching me intently as I recalled the details that led me to the woman I was supposed to love forever. I did love her. But according to her, I had a funny way of showing that shit. She was right. "When I saw that beautiful, milk chocolate skin and those locs she had in her hair, I grabbed my umbrella and went to save the day. I didn't speak. I just proceeded to help her get her groceries in the car while holding the umbrella over her. When we were done, we stood close, trying to get out of the rain. We were both soaked, but those slanted brown eyes had me stuck. I couldn't move or look away. It was the same way for her. After thanking me for my help, I gave her my phone number and asked her to call me. We ended up eating bland food that night because I went back to the trailer without the seasoning. Keisha was all I could think and talk about."

I closed my eyes and I felt disgusted with myself. That had been my sentiments for the past few years, but since Keisha left, I realized what that old saying meant. *You don't miss your water until your well runs dry.* I took advantage of her love and I was lucky that she stayed as long as she did. "So, when did things start to change?"

Without opening my eyes, I continued. "After my daughter was born," I sighed heavily, realizing I was gonna have to explain my foolish thinking in detail.

That thought alone worried the hell out of me. I hated these types of conversations. That was probably the main reason I was in the predicament I was in. The Hendersons were known for their outlandish behavior. My three younger siblings were bosses and didn't have a problem saying what they felt, especially Storm and Tiffany. Jasper didn't like expressing his personal life much, but since he'd been with Chasity, all that changed. WJ, Jenahra, and Chrissy, my older siblings, were pretty much the same way. Jenahra and Chrissy considered your feelings before they said what was needed to say.

Me? I didn't talk much at all, regardless of what it was about. I talked more around my family, because I couldn't help it around them, but to tell some stranger about all my downfalls was hard as hell. "Keisha wasn't feeling very sexual after the allotted time. We hadn't had sex since she was seven months pregnant, due to Karima trying to come early. Immediately after the six weeks, I was ready, and she shot me down. We'd never had sexual issues as long as we'd been together, but I didn't say anything. I knew she'd just had a baby and she probably wasn't ready."

After I didn't say anything else for a while, the therapist asked, "What happened?"

3

"After about six months of her only giving it to me sparingly, like once every two weeks, I started to notice other women. That made me feel like shit. I'm not at all blaming my wife... shit." I swallowed the lump in my throat, but that shit didn't help. A few tears graced my cheeks as I quickly wiped them away. "I'm not blaming my *ex-wife*. It was my decision to do the stupid-ass shit that I did."

"Just tell me how the first time happened and why it kept happening, and we'll be done for the day."

I slid my hands down my face. *Nothing worth having was easy. If you want your wife back, this is the first step to take getting there.* I closed my eyes once again. "It wasn't suddenly. This woman I remembered from high school had inboxed me on Facebook messenger, asking how I was doing and if I was still married. When I confirmed I was, the conversation didn't end. We had a few after that day and they were all innocent at first. You know... catching up. One day, she came to the convenience store and after scoping me out, the conversations turned sexual. It was subtle, but I caught where it was going."

"Why didn't you stop it?"

"Keisha and I hadn't had sex in over two months, and she seemed to be avoiding me. Karima was six months old and I was backed the fuck up. Jacking off wasn't helping. We were barely talking, and I hated that. Instead of voicing that to her, I talked to Shardae. It was easy, because Keisha wasn't the nagging type. She barely noticed *anything* I was doing around that time. After talking to Shardae for a month or so, I ended up meeting her. I don't have to say what happened after that."

"How did you feel after that?"

"I felt like shit. But when my needs got the best of me again, I forgot about how guilty I felt and did it again and again, until Shardae got pregnant for me. Which was strange in itself, because I always used condoms. She went to my house. I don't even know how she knew where I lived, but I guess she probably followed me. She told Keisha."

"How did that go?"

"She was hurt. I mean... we slept in separate rooms for at least a couple of weeks. I promised her it wouldn't happen again and apologized over and over. When she asked why I did it, I only said I didn't know. I didn't want to make her feel inadequate. I love Keisha... with all my heart. Although my act was disrespectful and made her feel unwanted and unloved, I didn't want to make her feel like it was her fault. After a month of apologizing and showering her with attention and gifts, she gave into me and we had sex. I was happy as shit, only for it to stop a week later, going back to what it was."

"And that was why you did it repeatedly?"

"Yeah, plus, it was out of habit. I'd gotten use to fucking around. I know I should have talked to her about it, but she had to know, right? She should have known that I wasn't okay with not being able to make love to my wife. Turning down my advances got old. I fucked around again... and again... and again."

"And she forgave you every time?"

"She only knows about another one, who also got pregnant. Shardae miscarried and I paid for Brandy to have an abortion. She saw me and Brandy at the clinic. And this last one... Tasha is still pregnant. She's almost halfway there and she's having a boy."

"Do you think you can go without sex?"

"I haven't had sex in over three months. It was hard not having sex when I had a wife laying next to me every night. I'd get so turned on watching her beautiful body, only to have to find someone else to help me relieve myself."

"You make it sound like you were urinating on them."

"They weren't my wife. So, it was random and meaningless... a lot like pissing. But it offered relief."

"Kendrall, what I'm not understanding is why do you want her back if you were so unsatisfied?"

I glanced at him for calling me by my full name when I clearly asked to be called Kenny. "After thinking over this, day in and day out, I believe Keisha was going through postpartum depression. I was too selfish and stupid to see it, then. But if we fucked like rabbits all those years before Karima, why would she suddenly stop? Then after my first infidelity... I could see why she didn't really wanna sleep with me. She didn't trust me."

Sliding my hands down my face, then bringing them back over my eyes, I said tearfully, "I ruined her. I betrayed her trust when she gave me no reason to. Instead of being there for my wife... my lover... my friend... the mother of my children, I turned my back on her and left her to deal with her issues alone. It's a miracle she didn't kill me. Why do I even think I deserve a second... shit, fifth chance at her heart? I need her and my kids... my babies. I miss my family."

I stood from my seat. I couldn't take any more of this shit. "Mr. Henderson? We still have ten minutes."

"Naw. We're good."

I walked out that bitch without looking back. He ain't do shit but get me all worked up about missing my family. And since I wasn't willing to tell him everything, this session wasn't going to help. No one knew everything about our marriage, but me... not even Keisha. After I got in my truck, I called Jasper. "Hello?"

"What's up, bruh?"

"Not much. Heading home. You a'ight?"

"Naw. You got some good shit?"

"Hell yeah. I always got some. You tryna smoke?"

"Yeah. I need something to level me out. I'm on my way. I ought to be there in fifteen minutes."

"A'ight."

I ended the call with him and looked at the time to see it was four o'clock. The kids were out of school. I called Keisha, wanting to hear their voices, including hers. When she answered, she didn't bother speaking. "They're doing homework, Kendrall. Focus on what other people have going on for a change. They'll call when they're done."

She ended the call before I could say a word. Yeah... I needed a fat ass blunt.

𝕶 I 𝕾

K enny
A year and a half later...

"DADDY, GOT'CHU, LIL MAN."

Kendrick had been crying almost non-stop. He was one year old, and he'd been in my custody for about four months. I believed he still missed his mama and had his moments. Tasha was a cold-ass bitch, though, and I hated I got caught up with her ass. I'd taken her to court to get full custody of him. When I went to her place to get him, she had shit everywhere. My son didn't need to be in that nasty ass environment. *What was I thinking, fucking with her?*

Just as I was walking around with him, the doorbell rang. I didn't know who it was, but I could use any help I could get. When I went to the door, Tiffany and Ryder stood there. They'd just gotten back from their honeymoon. We'd witnessed Tiffany win a national title for bare backing at the NFR and right after, they'd gon' to one of those Vegas chapels and scheduled a nice ass wedding. They'd been engaged for over a year and hadn't spoken of a wedding date because Tiffany was so involved with making it to the finals.

Tiffany immediately took Kendrick from me and he stopped crying. I rolled my eyes and offered them a seat. "Hey, Kenny. Seems like you're having a rough time."

"Seems? Ray Charles could see I was having a hard time and he's blind *and* dead."

She chuckled as Ryder shook my hand. "When did y'all get back?"

"Yesterday," Tiff said as Kendrick laid on her, content as hell. "Maybe he just needed a woman's touch. Or it could be because I'm pregnant."

I shrugged my shoulders, then wiped my hand down my face. Before I could offer them something to drink, my cell phone started ringing. "Hello?"

"Hey, Kendrall. Karima is sick, so they won't be able to make the trip. She's been throwing up and has a fever."

Ever since we'd broken up, Keisha had been calling me Kendrall. I didn't even care. I still loved her, and nothing would change that. "I hate to hear she's not feeling well. Is she up to talking?"

"She's asleep, but KJ is standing right here if you wanna talk to him."

"Yeah, please."

"Hey, Dad."

"Hey, son. How's it going?"

"It's going. I hate we can't come to Nome. Can you come to see us instead?"

"Let me talk to your mother."

I already knew this was gonna be a no go. Keisha had officially moved on with her life. She'd been dating this guy for about six months now, and the kids seemed to like him. The problem was that she never wanted to see me. So, the kids always had to fly to me. If they couldn't come for whatever reason, then I wouldn't see them.

One time, I'd flown out there and she wouldn't open the door. I was so pissed; I went to that grocery store we met at and just sat in the parking lot for hours.

Keisha literally hated me, and I got that. But I wished she would just let me be the father I was trying to be. I believed she was behaving that way because she still loved me. Seeing me would be hard for her. That was the only reason I didn't put up a fight. "Hello?"

"Hey. You think I can come see them?"

"No. That's not gonna work. Karima is sick, so that means you would have to come in my house. I've told you before that you aren't welcome inside my house."

"Fine. Well, you tell them why I can't come. When KJ asks me, I'm going to tell him why."

"Good. While you're at it, tell him how you were fucking random bitches while you were supposed to be married to me."

I breathed out hard and pinched the bridge of my nose. "Keisha. I just wanna see my babies. What I did has nothing to do with me being a father. I love my kids so much. I already can't see them all the time. If I don't see them this weekend, that'll be a month I've gone without them. I'm begging you."

"No. You weren't thinking about them and how a divorce would affect them when you were fucking around. In case you haven't noticed, I still hate you. Why would I make anything easy for you? Now if you're done, I have things to do."

She ended the call as Ryder and Tiffany stared at me. I looked at the phone for a moment, then threw that shit at the wall. What my life had become was a disgrace. Walking to my room, I flopped down on the bed, contemplating my next move. Did I wanna take a trip to San Antonio with my papers showing it was my weekend with the police in tow? Hell no. I wanted Keisha to stop being unreasonable. I wasn't hounding her as much about us getting back together, because she still hadn't forgiven me yet. Us getting back together would never happen at that rate.

I'd just been trying to focus on being a great dad to my children. I hated that Kendrick got to see me every day and they didn't. Tasha hadn't called but twice to check on him since I'd had him in my custody. She only wanted what she could get out me, not expecting me to want my kid. That was one thing I didn't inherit from my daddy. No matter how they got here, I loved my kids and they would know it, because I would be there for them.

Standing from my bed, I went to the bathroom and ran some water for Kendrick, then made my way back up front. Tiffany looked up at me with sad eyes. I didn't have to tell her what was going on. She knew the time I was having with Keisha. She wouldn't even answer Tiffany's phone calls anymore. She'd divorced the entire family. KJ had a phone, so I decided to call him on that. He usually got it taken away from him for cutting up in school. Dude was smart as a damn whip, but his attitude had gotten worse since they'd left Nome. He was already rowdy as hell, but the move made it worse. My kids were suffering without me, especially KJ, and I felt like it wasn't shit I could do about it. Just as I figured, the phone went straight to voicemail.

I grabbed Kendrick from Tiffany and she asked, "Kenny, you okay?"

I shook my head and quickly went to the bathroom. Tiffany seeing me this way was too much, so I surely didn't want Ryder all in my shit. I could hear them talking quietly as I undressed Kendrick for his bath. He was excited. He loved his baths. Pushing the duckies in the tub, I checked the temperature, then let him get in. He immediately began playing as my phone rang. It was WJ. I rolled my eyes. He irritated the fuck out of me at times, but whatever. "Hello?"

"Hey. You still have Price's number?"

"Daniels?"

"Yeah. How many men you know named Price?"

"Whatever. Yeah. Why?"

"I need a truck to haul this grass to Houston. Pete is having problems with the freightliner he was using."

"A'ight. I'll call him and tell him to call you."

Price was a good friend of mine. We'd met at LIT years ago when I was taking some business courses. He now owned his own trucking company, putting dump trucks, flatbeds and tankers on the road. He'd gotten married and, besides the daughter he was already raising, he'd had two more kids: twins. I shot him a text instead of calling. I really didn't feel like talking. *Hey bruh, can you call WJ? He wanted to get a bid on some work.*

I added the number, then looked at my phone. Keisha could kiss my ass. I was going to see my babies. I purchased a plane ticket to leave out tomorrow. As I bathed Kendrick, Tiffany came in the room. "We're gonna head to Storm's house. You coming?"

"For what?"

"They were barbequing for the family. You forgot?"

"Shit. Yeah, I did. Otherwise I wouldn't have bathed him right now. A'ight. When I get him out we'll head over there."

"Okay. Everything gon' be okay Kenny. You're a good man and I pray things get better soon."

"They have to, because I'm at the verge of crazy. I'm going back to that psychiatrist I was seeing. Too much shit is bothering me, and I hate feeling on edge all the time."

"Is it something you wanna talk to me about until you can get there? I don't mind listening, Kenny."

"Naw. You too opinionated. No offense. I love you, but there are some things I don't want my family to know about my marriage to Keisha."

She held her hands up. "Okay. Whatever you say. You need help with Kendrick?"

"I got him. Thanks, sis."

She kissed my cheek, then left out as I pulled a screaming Kendrick from the tub. This shit was getting old. I didn't know what else to do for him. It was like he hated me. As I held him in my arms with the towel wrapped around him, I said, "Ken, it's okay, man. Daddy got'chu. I'll always have you. You miss your mama, huh?"

He finally stopped screaming and looked at me. "Ma-ma."

I took a deep breath and rocked him. He was gonna have to see her eventually, but I didn't want him to. If she didn't get in touch with me to see him, though, that would be perfectly fine by me. I thought he would have forgotten her by now. It seemed I only got peace when he was asleep, eating, or around my family. And I didn't really get peace then. Keisha consumed my thoughts. The way she was trying to keep my kids from me was irritating the fuck out of me. There was so much more that she didn't think I knew about that I could hold over her head, but I refused to be that way. I had a good fucking heart, regardless of my fuck ups.

After getting Kendrick dressed and he realized we were leaving, he started smiling. He probably thought I was bringing him to his raggedy-ass mama. She was the reason I'd been celibate. I couldn't afford to fuck up with nobody else. With as much shit as I was going through, I still wanted Keisha back in my life. I'd give my right arm to go back and do things differently. I was almost sure that she would, too.

When we got to Storm's house, it sounded like somebody had released a damn zoo in there. I could hear kids screaming from outside. After walking inside, Kendrick immediately wanted out of my arms to run and play with the other kids. Once I put him down, I spoke to my family. I really didn't want to be there, and I guess I made that known by sitting in the corner. "Man, bring yo' miserable ass over here with everybody else," Storm yelled across the room.

I rolled my eyes as everyone else laughed. *Fuck them.* Instead of going to them, I decided to carry my ass back home. I went picked Kendrick up and was trying to leave as he threw a fit. "Kenny, why are you leaving?" my mama asked.

"I just don't feel like joking around, Ma."

"Leave the baby here. We'll bring him home."

Releasing Kendrick to go back and play, I took off out the door. "Kenny! You know I was just fucking wit'chu. Where you going?"

"Home."

Storm caught up with me and stood in front of me. "You have to face facts, bruh. Life goes on. You been pining over Keisha's ass for over a year. You fucked up, but most likely, she ain't cutting for your ass no more. You have to move on."

"I can't."

"I get that she was perfect and shit, but why can't you let go?"

"She was far from perfect, but I love her."

What possessed me to say that shit to Storm, I didn't know. Because he was gon' be all in my business now until I told him. "Aww shit. What the fuck Keisha did?"

"None of your business, Storm. Now, I'm going home and get right."

"Hell naw, nigga. That's the problem. You always running from shit. Keep fucking with me. I'm gon' get all the secrets out. You won't need to pay a therapist. Make sure you make the check out to Seven, not Storm."

I rolled my eyes. "I'm not running. I just don't feel like airing out our dirty laundry. It's bad enough y'all know a lot of it. I don't feel like I ever fit in around y'all anyway. You, Jasper and Tiffany pushed me out, and Jenahra, WJ, and Chrissy did the same. All I got is me and sometimes Shylou."

Shylou was co-owner of the convenience store, but I was in the process of getting a loan to buy him out. He was tired of the business. I didn't blame him. He was from Houston, so this country pace was killing him. He'd been coming here every weekend from Houston for almost ten years and was a groomsman in my wedding, along with Price and my three brothers. "Man, I oughta knock you on yo' ass. You know got damn well we here for you if you need us. Whether it's to have your back or fuck you up. Now be a Henderson and man up!"

"Man get the fuck outta my face with that shit!"

In my peripheral, I saw Jasper, Ryder, and WJ coming outside to get in between me and Storm. Just because he was tall as fuck didn't mean I wouldn't knock his big ass out. He didn't know how to leave well-enough alone. "Kenny, until you can own up to all the shit you did, ain't shit gon' ever be right in your life. Yo' shit is all fucked up."

"I owned up to my shit! But I ain't the only muthafucka that was wrong!"

I got in my truck, because I was getting dangerously close to spilling some tea that was gon' fuck all of them up.

2

K eisha

"MOMMY, IS DADDY GONNA COME SEE ME WHILE I'M SICK?"

"No, baby. Just concentrate on feeling better. You'll be able to go to Nome next time."

I rubbed her head, then went back to the front room with Bashir. We'd been dating for six months and things were going great. We had our minor hiccups, but what couple didn't? He came over every evening for at least an hour when he got off work. With all the money my ex-husband was sending, I didn't have to work. I made sure that he understood that I wouldn't be taking him back. So, if he wanted to continue paying for everything, that was on him. He only had to send $2,200 a month for his child support payments.

He filed on himself, knowing that I probably would. And he was right in that assumption. I pretty much got everything I wanted. The only thing I didn't fight him for was the house. He could have it. I was getting enough money from him already. The only thing I would do with the house was sell it anyway, because I could never live there again. I couldn't even stand the thought of Kenny, and that house held plenty of memories: good and bad.

When I sat next to Bashir, he kind of nudged me away. "You gon' make me lose. KJ ain't gon' beat me this time."

I rolled my eyes. Those two were so competitive when it came to that damn game. That was one of our minor hiccups. Sometimes he spent more time playing the game with KJ than he spent with me. Huffing loudly, I went to the kitchen to start putting food away. If only Kenny could have kept his dick in his pants, my life would have been perfect. It was one of the reasons why I couldn't stand his guts now. Had it not been for that, he would have been perfect. He was an amazing provider and a wonderful father. When he was home, I had his undivided attention. Even when I felt like I didn't deserve his undivided attention, he gave it to me unconditionally.

Sometimes I questioned whether I had made the right decision, but then most times, I knew if I wouldn't have left, the behavior would have continued. It was a miracle that he never brought me any STD's. Our lives were so perfect until I had Karima. Shaking my head of my thoughts, I continued putting food away and putting the dishes in the dishwasher. "Babe, I'm gonna head out on a high note. I finally beat KJ."

"Are you serious?" I asked as I turned to him.

He was indeed serious. There he stood with his keys in his hand. "Yeah, baby. I'm tired. I been working all day. I just wanna go take a shower and go to bed. Thank you for dinner."

He kissed my cheek as I silently fumed. I refused to go through the same bullshit I went through with Kenny. We were definitely gonna talk. Whenever he wanted to fuck, he was gon' get an earful. I didn't bother to walk him out. As I finished loading the dishwasher, KJ walked in the kitchen. "Why you told Dad not to come?"

"KJ, I don't feel like having this conversation tonight."

"Then when we gon' have it? Just 'cause you divorced him don't mean me and Karima gotta divorce him, too."

"Bring yo' ass to bed, lil boy. Remember, I'm yo' mama and I will bust yo' ass. Watch how you talk to me. Understood?"

"Yeah."

"Yeah? You wanna run that by me again?"

He huffed. "Yes, ma'am."

When he walked out of the kitchen, I rolled my eyes. Looking up to the ceiling, I counted to ten. I knew he was right, but I couldn't handle seeing Kenny. I knew he still loved me, and under all the anger and hurt, I still loved him, too. I'd met him right out of high school, and he'd been my everything. Seeing him for an extended amount of time would eventually wear me down. Ever since we'd been here in San Antonio, I'd had problems with KJ being disrespectful. I knew it was because I left their dad, but he couldn't begin to understand, and I didn't expect him to. He was only thirteen.

After I finished the kitchen, I went to my room to take a shower and go to bed. I was tired. Today was laundry day and I'd cleaned up. Taking care of a sick child was tiring in itself, though. Before I could get in the shower, my phone was ringing. When I saw Kenny's number, I huffed loudly and ignored his call. It rang again right after. Kendrall Henderson. He knew I would get tired before he did, and it was crazy that we played this game all the damn time. I didn't know why he couldn't respect the fact that I didn't want to talk to him. "What, Kendrall?"

"I'll be there at nine tomorrow morning. I need to see my kids, Keisha."

"And what did I tell you? I told you Karima was sick!"

He remained quiet for a moment, then said in a deep tone. "I'm not going to allow you to keep my kids from me. Don't make me get the police involved."

My eyebrows lifted in surprise. "I've had enough, Keisha. I need to see my babies, and I'm not finna let you or nobody else keep me from my kids. Karima doesn't have to leave her bedroom, but I need

17

to see them. If that means I sit in her room or lay in bed with her, then so be it. They need their father and I'm not finna let you fuck my kids up, making them think I don't wanna be a part of their lives. You said you moved on, then prove it. Obviously, you haven't if you still that fucking angry. Nine o'clock, LaKeisha."

He ended the call and my mouth was hanging open. Kenny had never spoken to me so roughly. I wanted to call him back and curse him out, but I decided to leave it alone. He wouldn't get away with that bullshit next time, though. I got in the shower and allowed the hot water to wash away my anger and frustration with Bashir and Kenny. As I washed, I could hear my phone ringing again. I rolled my eyes, knowing it was one of the two of them and I was leaning more towards Kenny.

When I got out of the shower and had dried off, the fucking phone started ringing again. I wanted to just turn the shit off. Just as I figured, it was Kenny. "You have more you need to demand of me?"

"I'm sorry, Keisha. It's just... I've already lost you. I can't lose my kids, too. I'm supposed to see them every other weekend and for the entire summer and one week of the winter break. You know that. I hate myself for the shit I've done, but my kids are my lifelines. I can't live without seeing my kids. Every two weeks is hard enough, but I look forward to taking my mind off my troubles and enjoy being with them. Don't take that from me. Please."

I dropped a couple of tears, but I would never admit that to him. "Okay, Kenny. When you get here, I'll leave you here with them."

"You don't have to leave, Keisha."

"Yes, I do. I hate you and I can't stand to be in the same room with you. It's hard enough talking to you on the phone. Are you done?"

"Yeah. Sorry."

I ended the call and laid in my bed naked for a moment. It took effort to be rude to Kenny. I knew the start of his sleeping around wasn't totally on him, but at the same time, he should have come and talked to me before fucking somebody else. *Maybe I should have talked to him.* There were so many what if's, until it practically justified another chance, but I knew I couldn't raise another woman's child. No matter how much I loved him, that was something I refused to do. I got up and moisturized my skin, then put on some pajamas and went checked on Karima. When I cracked the door open, I saw that she was sound asleep.

KJ was still playing the game. I could hear it. I walked up front and said, "Turn it down some and be sure to get some rest. Your dad will be here at nine."

His eyes brightened and were wide as saucers. "Really, Mom?"

"Really."

"I'm going to bed now so tomorrow can hurry and get here."

He turned off the TV and walked toward me. When he got to me, I expected him to keep walking, but instead, he hugged me tightly. "Thank you for telling him he could come."

I didn't bother enlightening him by saying it wasn't my decision. He looked at me as the enemy and for once I wasn't that. I kissed his head and said, "Goodnight, son."

"Goodnight, Mom."

Going back to my room, I laid down and stared at the ceiling, knowing I wouldn't get much sleep. I hadn't seen Kenny in months, and I would have to see him tomorrow. My nerves were getting the best of me and my stomach was in knots. I got back up and went to the kitchen and fixed me a drink. It was actually a shot of Henny. I tossed it back, then poured another and tossed it back as well. Walking back to my room, I knew that was a waste of time, because nothing could have me numb enough to where I wouldn't feel Kenny's soul.

⚘

WHEN I HEARD, *WHAT'S UP, DAD,* I KNEW I'D OVERSLEPT. *SHIT!* I hopped out of bed and handled my hygiene, then quickly got dressed. Pulling my dreads up in a ponytail, I applied a little makeup,

19

then grabbed my purse to head out. As soon as I stepped out in the hallway, my eyes met his. *Why did he have to look so damn good?* He only wore a t-shirt and some jeans, but shit. He could wear whatever the fuck he wanted. His hair was wild and untamed, looking like the damn king of the jungle, calling out to his lioness.

We were both staring at one another and my heartrate had risen to dangerous speeds. "Hey, Keisha," he said in that baritone voice that I loved.

"Hey."

I quickly tried to brush by him, but he grabbed my hand. The heat that coursed through my body was unwelcomed, and I couldn't control it. No matter what Kenny did, I'd always love him, because his heart was gold. We never sat and really talked about why he did the things he did after the first time. We were both shy about expressing our feelings to one another... well, mainly the confrontational ones. Had this fuckery with Tasha not gotten out, I would probably still be with him.

We should have communicated more, gone to counseling, or anything after the first chick. Postpartum depression wasn't a joke, and had I talked to him about it, I knew he would have understood. How did I expect him to understand if I didn't talk about it? My doctor had diagnosed me with it after I told him how I was feeling. I knew a lot of men didn't really understand it. So, it was my job to tell him, but I kept my mouth closed, pushing my husband away. Thinking he would just know that something was wrong when I didn't want him was the wrong thing to assume. Everything that happened afterwards stemmed directly from my omission.

I tried to jerk away from him, but he didn't let go. KJ was watching us so closely, I didn't wanna say anything to have him hating me more. "Keisha, can we talk? Just for a moment."

I huffed. "KJ go to your room for a minute."

He took off with a smile on his face. This was the first time he'd witnessed me succumbing to Kenny. We walked to the front room and sat on the couch. God, I wanted to grab handfuls of his hair while he made love to me. I had to be crazy. He grabbed my hand and said, "Can we come to some kind of agreement about the kids? I know this is on me, but you have to admit that I do everything I can for my kids... and for you."

He lifted his hand and gently rubbed his fingers down my cheek. I leaned away from his touch. "We can go back to how things were. If there is ever a conflict, I'll let you know as soon as I can so different arrangements can be made. That good enough for you?"

He tilted his head slightly and stared at me as his eyebrows scrunched together, giving me that puppy dog look that always made me weak. I looked away from him and stood from the couch, going to the kitchen. I was about to hightail it out of here and hadn't checked on Karima or given her any medicine. Kenny had me all flustered and he knew it. I could barely focus on what I was doing. "Keisha, can we go to counseling and get all this shit out? I went alone, but I think it will benefit us if we went together."

"It would only benefit us if there was a chance of us getting back together. I'm done, Kendrall. I've been telling you that for over a year. I can't go through that hurt again."

"You don't think I'm hurt?"

I frowned as I stared at him. It felt like his gaze was penetrating my very being... like he could see my thoughts and my heart. My nerves kicked up a notch as I brushed past him once again, heading to Karima's room. She was awake but staring off into nothingness until she caught a glimpse of Kenny. She sprang from the bed and yelled, "Daddy! You came!"

"Of course, I did! How's my baby feeling?" he asked as he lifted her in his arms with a bright smile on his face.

Karima played in his hair and she said, "Better, now that you're here. Where's Kendrick?"

"He stayed with Grandma and Grandpa. I thought I needed to spend time with just the two of y'all. I miss y'all so much."

At that point, I had to leave the room. The lump in my throat was threatening to take me down. As I did, my phone rang. It was my best friend, Cass. "Hello?"

"Girl, where the hell you at? I'm sitting here in Starbucks waiting on your ass."

"I'm on my way, Cass."

"Uh huh. Kenny done got ahold to that ass. I don't know why you being stubborn."

"Because he was fucking around, Cass! Did you forget?"

"Nope. But yo' ass ain't innocent. Did *you* forget?"

I closed my eyes and exhaled my frustrations. "I'll be there in a lil bit," I said and ended the call.

Going back to the room, I found Kenny sitting on the floor with Karima, having a tea party. My heart was so full. This was one of the reasons I didn't want him here. "Come on, baby, and take this medicine."

Karima bounced to her feet and took her antibiotics and Motrin, then flopped back to the floor with her daddy. He stared up at me for a moment, and I knew I had to get out of there. "I'll see you guys later."

"Okay! Bye Mommy!"

Walking down the hallway, I almost ran into KJ as he came out of his room. "Thanks again, Mom."

"You're welcome," I said as I tried to get out the door before the tear fell.

K enny

SEEING MY KIDS HAD ME EMOTIONAL AS HELL, BUT I COULDN'T let them see that. Just since I'd been here, Karima seemed to be doing so much better. I'd fixed her some soup and she drank a Sprite, while KJ and I played one of his video games. I hated video games, but I could never tell my son that. I enjoyed spending time with them, no matter what we were doing. Once Karima was done with her soup, I read the instructions on her antibiotics and gave her another dose. Once we went back to her room, I laid in bed with her. "Daddy, I wish we could move back to Nome."

"Me too, baby. I hate not seeing y'all every day, but it's my fault. I hurt your mother and she's still hurting because of some of the things I did. Just know that I love y'all so much and I'll do whatever I have to do to see y'all. This every-two-weeks is killing me. I'm gonna talk to your mama about y'all coming to me one weekend and I come to y'all the next. That way we don't have to go so long without seeing one another."

"Okay. I hope she says yes."

"Me too. Get some rest, baby."

I held my daughter in my arms and sang one of her favorite songs to her, "Rock with You" by Michael Jackson. I sang it at a slower tempo as she drifted off. These were the times I missed with my baby. When I got up and had left the room, I called my mama to check on Kendrick. "Hello?"

"Hey, Ma. I was calling to check on Kendrick. How is he?"

"He's fine, baby. He's playing with Bali, Noni, Ashanni and Royal."

That was Storm and Jasper's girls and Jasper's son. Kendrick seemed to be perfectly fine when he was with anyone else. Maybe it *was* me. He hated me. But he was a baby. He didn't know what it meant to hate, so I didn't know what to think of it. "Okay. I need to talk to you when I get back. Okay?"

"Okay, baby. How's Karima and KJ?"

"They're missing me as much as I miss them. I wish I could at least get Keisha to move back."

"I know, baby. Don't give up. I know it seems hopeless, but never give up on something you want. Continue to work on yourself... become a better person and strive for peace in all facets of your life. You will be victorious. King David made all sorts of bad decisions, but he was the apple of God's eye. There's hope despite what you've been through. And I can't wait to see where God elevates you to after all this is said and done."

"Thank you, Mama. Those words of encouragement mean so much to me. It feels good that someone is rooting for me. Now, I have to call Storm and apologize."

She chuckled. "That knucklehead is outside with your daddy, repairing fence, but I'm sure he has that thing on his head."

"Okay, Mama. I love you."

IN WAY TOO DEEP

"I love you, too, baby."

I ended the call with her and felt renewed. It felt like I was spinning my wheels, but I was wearing Keisha down. I had to be. Taking a deep breath, I decided to order pizza for KJ first, then I would call bullheaded Storm. I knew he meant well last night, and he was right with most of what he said. Once they confirmed the pizza would be delivered in twenty to thirty minutes, I called Storm. "Yeah?"

"I apologize. You were right. I do a lot of running. But... that doesn't mean I need to share all the details of my marriage with y'all."

Truth was, if they knew about some of the things Keisha did, they wouldn't be as forgiving. I was their brother... big difference. I loved her despite the bullshit and she and I needed to talk about everything I knew that she didn't think I knew. "Long as you talk to somebody, bruh. I apologize, too, for trying to bully you into saying something."

"Well, shit. What did I do to deserve an apology from the Storm?"

He laughed. "And you betta not tell nobody."

I laughed, too. "I realized that you were right about what you said. We did push you out of our lil clique. All of us did. We made you feel like you didn't belong."

"It's cool, Storm. We're good."

"Well, how are things going out there?"

"They're good."

"I miss those Tasmanian Devils."

I chuckled. KJ was a handful when he was little. "Shit!"

"What happened?"

"I stuck my finger with this barbed wire. I'll talk to you later."

"A'ight. But you need to wear gloves."

"Fuck that. I'm the Storm, baby. Ain't nothing soft about me but my hair. I'll hit'chu later."

I shook my head as he ended the call, then made some business calls. The loan was still being processed. I didn't know why they were dragging their feet about it. I planned to add on to the store as well. I wanted to eventually make it a truck stop. That would bring plenty of revenue and I also wanted to start an ambulance service. When the pizza got to the house, KJ was ready and hell, I was, too. I was starving. Rushing to the airport, I didn't have time to get breakfast. Ryder gave me a lift since he had to go to Baytown. It wasn't too far past his destination.

KJ was practically inhaling his pizza, since he hadn't eaten breakfast, either. "Dad? What happened between you and Mama exactly? I been trying to piece together the parts I heard. You cheated on Mama?"

I exhaled hard. I should have known this would come eventually. He was getting older. "Yeah, I did. It was wrong and I regret it so much. I love your mama and I can't even explain why that happened. I was stupid, selfish, and just... wasn't thinking about the long-term consequences of my actions. Like not being able to see y'all every day."

"So, Mama has a reason to be pissed whenever your name comes up?"

"Yeah but watch your mouth."

"So, why can't y'all work this out? It's been almost two years since we moved. I hate it here. I'd rather be cutting cows or mowing hay fields. This city life is for the birds."

I wanted to laugh but he was dead serious. "I'm trying to work things out with your mom. I hurt her bad and having Kendrick only makes it worse. He's a daily reminder of my infidelity. I'm being patient with her. But... we may never get back together. If we can at least be friends and I could get her to move closer, then I'll be satisfied."

Who was I kidding? I was gonna go to my grave trying to prove my love to her. That was why I was paying for everything. She didn't have to work when she was mine and she didn't have to work now. Keisha hadn't had a job since she was a teenager. So, she depended on me financially. The only problem that I had was another nigga benefitting from my generosity. If he so much as got his belly full, he was benefitting from my money. I supplied everything in this condo, from the condo itself, to a grain of rice.

KJ continued eating as I started to pick over my supreme pizza. Talking about our situation caused me to lose my appetite. "Let's just enjoy our time today and tomorrow."

"Yes, sir."

As I forced myself to take another bite of pizza, there was a knock at the door. I frowned slightly, then looked at KJ. "Y'all expecting anybody?"

"Probably Bashir. He pops up sometimes."

I finally get to meet this dude that's been around my kids. Going to the door, I swung it open as I looked down on him. I wasn't as tall as my brothers, but compared to him, I was a giant. I was six-three, so he had to be like five-ten or so. He tried looking past me as I frowned. I didn't care if he was a cop or not. "Umm, I'm Bashir, Keisha's boyfriend. You must be Kendrall."

"Kenny."

"My bad. The kids look just like you. Is Keisha around?"

"Naw. She's been gone all day."

"Oh okay. Had I known you were going to be here, I would have called first. I didn't mean to interrupt your time with the kids."

"No problem."

He seemed like a cool guy. When he walked away, I closed the door, then turned back to KJ. "Does he treat y'all good?"

"Yes, sir. He plays the game with me a lot."

"How does he treat your mom?"

He shrugged his shoulders. "They don't seem to talk that much, unless they talk when they go in her room."

I was sure my face had turned red. They were talking alright. I knew that KJ knew exactly what was going on in that room. He didn't have to admit that he did, and I wasn't gon' press because I didn't wanna talk about the shit. Grabbing my pizza from the bar area, I closed the box and sat it on the stove for later as KJ asked, "Will we get to go hang out, Dad? Shoot some hoops or something?"

"Maybe. If your mom comes back before it gets dark."

I sat in the recliner while KJ laid on the sofa and put on a movie we used to watch together all the time. *Cool Runnings*. "I haven't watched this in over two years."

"I watch it almost every weekend when we aren't with you. It was our movie."

"Yeah," I said under my breath.

I had to get them back to Nome. No ifs, ands, or buts about it.

We'd been watching the movie for an hour, when I heard KJ snoring. Slightly shaking my head, I smiled at my namesake. He was even growing his hair out so he could be like me. I was surprised Keisha was allowing him to do that. Turning the movie off, I went to the room to check on Karima and she was still asleep. After closing her door, I slid down to the floor and prayed that God would restore me and put me and Keisha on the road to healing. We needed this so badly. I could see how nervous she got when I was staring at her earlier. She still thought I didn't know.

Resting my head on my knees, I prayed until I ran out of words. All I could get out was, *please*. My phone vibrated in my pocket and I realized it was a text from Keisha. *How's Karima?*

She's asleep, so is KJ.

I remained on the floor, waiting to see if she would say anything else. After a minute or so, she asked, *Does Karima need more Tylenol?*

I smirked. She knew whether Karima had enough medicine or not. She just wanted to keep messaging me. *Yeah, she does.* I kept my response short, only answering her questions. I allowed my mind to travel back in time, thinking about the last time we were happy... six years ago. Karima was a baby and we'd decided to go for a walk at the park. KJ was seven and he was excited to get out of the house. We'd been cooped up for a couple of days because of the rain. Karima was only a month old. We were walking around the waterspout and I guess I'd gotten too close. That shit came on and drenched me and Keisha. Thankfully none got on Karima, because of the covering on her stroller. We laughed all the way home about it. That was truly the last time I remembered laughing with my wife.

I stood from the floor and walked to the kitchen. Peeping over at KJ to see he was still asleep, I put in a call to the psychiatrist. It was past time.

4

K eisha

"I DON'T KNOW WHY YOU DON'T JUST COME CLEAN. ALL HIS SHIT is out in the open for the world to judge, but you still harboring secrets and shit like ain't shit happen. I get that you did that shit in retaliation, but you still did it and maintained the shit for years. How dare you throw stones at that man?"

"He started the shit, Cass. He did it first. There's nothing he can tell me about shit, when he's the one that opened that pandora's box."

"You a fucking hypocrite. If you forgave him after that first time, you are *not* justified in what you did. If you didn't forgive him, then you should have left. You and Reggie had an entire fucking affair for four years. And you probably still fucking him occasionally. I don't understand you. Then on top of that shit, you know that he's your sister-in-law's ex-boyfriend. How you think she gon' feel about that shit?"

"She's gonna be upset about me cheating, regardless of who it's with. Reggie doesn't want the commitment. Neither do I. So, he was perfect for what I used his ass for."

"Keisha, if you could only hear how the fuck you sound. How do you get angry about the second, third, fuck... the tenth infidelity if you fucking around, too? Whether you with the same nigga or not, you were still fucking around. If anything, yours was worse!"

My eyebrows furrowed as I stared at her. "How you figure?"

"You established a fucking relationship with that nigga. Kenny was just busting a nut, since his fucking wife was unavailable to him sexually. It makes me wonder if he knows about your shit. That's probably why he kept fucking around on you."

"If he knew, Cass, why wouldn't he say something?"

"Shit, that's a good question. Maybe because he loves your triflin' ass."

I frowned at her again and before I could respond to her, she said, "I already see your wheels turning and you ready to get all defensive and shit. But listen. Kenny was wrong for cheating. But... what you wanted that man to do? His own fucking wife refused to screw him for months and didn't bother telling him why. I came close to telling him myself. Kenny loves you so damn much. He allowed you to mistreat him and never asked why. Not that this is an excuse, but I'm willing to bet that he didn't think about cheating until that chick came along. I'm also willing to bet that she made the first move sexually."

I rolled my eyes. I knew she had a point. However, admitting shit that no one had to know was out of the question. I didn't cheat until he did. No one would blame me for that. When I didn't respond to her verbally, she continued, "So, save that fucking sob story for somebody that don't know all your shit. Say what you want, but *you* responsible for the cracks in your marriage. *You* ushered the destruction in. *You* pushed him away. Now fuck wit' it. I'm done and ain't shit you can say to dispute anything I've said, so you might as well sulk and eat that pitiful-ass bagel."

As she drank her latte, my phone rang. It was Bashir. Before answering, I said, "And for the record, I'm no longer fucking Reggie... just Bashir."

I answered the call and brought the phone to my ear. "Hello?"

"Hey, baby. Why you didn't tell me you wouldn't be home?"

"I'm sorry. It was a last-minute decision late last night and I woke up late this morning. I apologize."

"I met your ex."

"And?"

"He seems kind of rude. Did he know about me?"

"Yeah. How was he rude?"

"Well... not really rude. He just didn't have much to say."

"He's always that way. It has nothing to do with you."

"Well, can I see you today? Will he be staying at your place?"

"No. Even if that's his plans, he gotta go. He cannot stay with me."

I glanced over at Cass to see the frown on her face. "Nigga can stay wherever the fuck he want, since he paying for the shit," she mumbled.

I rolled my eyes. "You can come over, Bashir, but we need to talk."

"About what?"

"You'll see when you get there."

"A'ight. Guess I better be on guard in case you wanna chop a nigga up."

"Whatever. I'm out with Cass. I'll call you back."

I ended the call before he had a chance to respond and thought about everything Cass had said. There was no way I could tell Kenny about my indiscretions. If he knew and wasn't saying anything, then that was on him. If he wasn't going to confront me about it, then why should I bring it up? As I took a sip of my coffee, I got a text from Kenny. *When you get here, you think you can braid my hair? It's curlier than what I like it to be.*

I already knew I wouldn't be able to handle him sitting between my legs. I could barely handle the thought of it. I texted back, *No*.

Not giving him any more of an answer than that, I took another sip of my coffee while Cass watched me. "You're right, shit. Quit looking at me like that. But I ain't telling Kenny shit."

"I didn't say you had to tell him, but you ain't gotta treat him like shit, either, when yo' ass is just as guilty."

Kenny was gonna think something was up and that I was ready to get back together if I suddenly started being nice to him. Maybe I could gradually get there. When he stared at me earlier, it felt like he knew something he wasn't saying, though. Kenny was a very mild-mannered person and it took a lot to set him off. But for some reason, I felt like he was getting close to that breaking point. I'd kept up this angry, spiteful attitude with him for so long, though, it would take practice to change it.

As I finally finished my bagel, I noticed Cass had been watching me, so I decided to speak up. "You're right. I've been a horrible person to him. I know I'm not a saint. But I *am* still angry with him."

"Keisha, listen. I'm gon' say this shit again. I don't condone cheating. Kenny was wrong as hell. But! You denying that man, pushed him to seek it elsewhere. Ain't shit worse than laying next to a muthafucka that's supposed to be your life partner and feel a disconnection. The worst part is that you didn't tell him what was going on with you. Is he a mind reader? Hell naw. Should he have asked? Maybe. But it was on you to tell him. His actions were a reaction to your behavior. That's all I'm saying. So, if you're angry with him, then you should be angry with yourself, too, boo."

"Maybe I am angry with myself. But there's nothing I can do to take shit back."

"And that goes for Kenny. He can't take any of that shit back, either."

I clasped my hands together in front of my face for a moment, then stood to throw my trash away. When I sat, Cass said, "Let's go watch a movie to mellow your ass out before you go home to at least be somewhat friendly with Kenny."

I rolled my eyes, then followed her out the door. I suppose catching a matinee wouldn't be a bad idea. Maybe then, I could braid Kenny's hair without feeling a type of way. If we could develop a true friendship, things could get better between us. Besides, it's been almost two years since I left him. "Although I've already seen it, let's go watch The Photograph."

"Oh, hell yeah. That'll mellow yo' ass out," Cass snapped. "If that shit had me crying, I already know that's gon' damn near have you ready to say fuck it all and give into Kenny."

I again rolled my eyes at her retarded ass and got in my car, secretly hoping she was right.

⚜

When I got home, my feelings were all over me. I was feeling so sensitive, I knew I would cry at the first sight of Kenny. Thankfully, Bashir showed up at the same time I did. After getting out of my car, I waited for him to do the same. "I thought I was supposed to call you when I got home?"

"You were, but I was somewhat anxious to hear what you had to say."

I took a deep breath and exhaled, then nodded. As I walked to the condo, Bashir grabbed my hand and stopped me. "A kiss would be nice. I'm starting to think this conversation won't be a good one."

I smiled softly at him, then laid my lips on his gently. Pulling me closer to him by my waist, he deepened the kiss. *Shit. What conversation?* It was bad enough I was feeling sensitive. Now all I wanted to do was make love to Bashir. I had to admit that his dick game was amazing, but it wasn't nearly as essential as Kenny's. The more I saw him, the more I realized how much I needed him... not to mention his dick and his finances. Kenny gave me the world, and at this point, I was accepting the gift as if I deserved it.

Bashir's hands slid down to my ass, breaking my thoughts about Kenny. The way he cupped and squeezed my ass cheeks had me beyond ready. His fingertips had grazed my pussy, awakening her even more than she already was. Slowly pulling away from him without a word, I grabbed his hand and led him to the condo. When I put my key in the lock, I noticed my trembling hand. *Why was I so fucking nervous?* Quickly turning the lock before Bashir noticed it, I opened the door to see Kenny and KJ sitting on the floor on either side of the coffee table, engaged in a game of Connect Four, while Karima sat on the sofa behind Kenny, playing in his hair.

I smiled at the sight and realized how much I missed it. My heart had turned to mush, seeing the bows and barrettes Karima had adorned him with. *What was I doing?* My babies needed their dad. As the lump formed in my throat, they all looked over at me and Bashir. "Hey Mommy! I feel so much better!" Karima yelled.

"I see! That's amazing!"

Kenny was only staring at me and Bashir. I'd almost forgotten he was even with me until he rested his hand on my hip. Kenny brought my attention back to him when he said, "I wanna take them to dinner. Can you comb Karima's hair?"

I nodded and said, "Come on, baby. Let's get you dressed."

Bashir followed me down the hallway, so I said, "You can wait for me in my room."

He looked me up and down and said, "Mmm hmm."

Karima frowned for a moment, but I gently pushed her in her room before she could say anything. After we found her something cute to wear and dressed her, Kenny was standing in the doorway with her hairbows and barrettes. I took them from him without a word and he walked away. "Mommy? Why is Bashir here while Daddy is here? You don't wanna spend time with Daddy?"

"Your dad is here to spend time with you and KJ, not me, sweetheart. Remember I explained to you that he and I were no longer married or together?"

"Yes ma'am," she said sadly.

She had a head full of hair just like her dad. It was soft and extremely manageable. When I'd finished combing her hair, I led her out to Kenny and KJ. They were seated on the couch and I noticed Kenny had changed and pulled his hair up into a man bun. *God, why was he so damn sexy?* "Aww, you so pretty, Rima," he said as his face became animated just like hers.

She smiled and twirled around with her arms outstretched, then ran to him. He picked her up and kissed her cheek. "Thank you, Daddy."

I swallowed hard as he put her down and looked at me. "We should be back in three hours or so. Can we use your car?"

"That would leave me stranded, Kenny."

"Isn't Bashir here?" KJ asked. "He can bring you wherever you need to go."

Kenny looked over at him but didn't say a word about him jumping in our conversation. When Kenny turned back to me, there was ice in his glare. That shit stunned me. "Don't worry about it. I'll get an Uber," he said.

I was uncomfortable as hell as he stared at me. His breaking point would happen soon. I got that vibe just from staring at him, noticing his fuck-it-all demeanor. I quickly nodded and went to the kitchen to escape his scrutiny. Getting a bottle of water from the fridge, I heard him tell the kids, "Let's go have a good time. Karima, let's get you a jacket with a hood, baby girl."

I watched her lead Kenny to her room, and they came out with her favorite jacket with the fur around the hood. He glanced at me once more and nodded. I was nervous as hell, because I'd never seen him this way. His calm demeanor was slipping from his grasp and I could only hope that he could pull it back before they got back home. "Bye, Mommy!" Karima yelled.

"Bye. Y'all have a good time."

They walked out the door, so I went to and locked it. I peeped through the peephole to see Karima on Kenny's shoulders and KJ smiling. I hadn't seen his smile in two weeks, when they were boarding on their flight to go see Kenny. I turned and leaned against the door as feelings of inadequacy flooded my being. I quickly checked myself, though. Just because they wanted to be with their dad more, didn't mean they didn't want me. They just wanted us both at the same time, like it used to be.

Forcing myself away from the door, I trudged down the hallway to my bedroom. Bashir and I would probably have that talk anyway, because fucking was the last thing on my mind now. When I entered the room, he was lying in the bed in his drawers and my eyes immediately went to his hard dick. *On second thought...*

I closed and locked the door. That was out of habit. I took off my clothes as I made my way to him and watched him shed the drawers he was wearing. I immediately climbed on top of him and let his dick touch those sensitive areas inside of me. "Damn, Keisha. What did you wanna talk about, though?"

"Mmm. How... I want your attention... even when we aren't fucking."

I rolled my hips on his dick with my eyes closed, but still thinking about Kenny. I couldn't get him off my mind. The way he looked at me before he left, had shaken me to my core. His other brothers all could have bad tempers at times, and he reminded me of his youngest brother for a moment. That scowl that was a permanent fixture on Storm's face had now graced his gorgeous face. His Henderson side was about to make an appearance and, although I was nervous about it, it was turning me on at the same time.

I'd blocked out Bashir's voice and all I heard was Kenny's smooth Baritone, begging me to be his again. We were more alike than I cared to admit and while that contributed to our demise, it also added to our chemistry. Before all this drama, we got along perfectly. I handled everything around the house and actually enjoyed doing it while he took care of us financially. I knew he had a lot on his plate with the rice fields and his store, so I did what I could and searched You Tube for instruction on how to fix the things I thought I couldn't.

Bashir's grunts brought me back to the present. He grabbed my hips and said, "Fuck! You got all my attention right now, though. I'll do better."

His hands slid up my body to my nipples and he gently pinched each pierced one, causing me to cum on his dick. "Bash... Shit!"

He flipped me over, interrupting my orgasmic wave and hooked my leg with his arm, bringing it to my shoulder and started digging me out. I tilted my head back and he rested his other hand on my neck, applying slight pressure. "Keisha, tell me you love this dick."

I licked my lips and imagined it was Kenny's dick to get me through the moment. I thought I would be able to handle his request if I did. But I soon realized there was no way I could tell him that honestly. When I remained quiet, he started stroking me deeper and rougher, but it still produced no sound out of me, just slight moans from the air being forced out of me because of the pressure of his strokes. "Keisha... I love your pussy, baby. You don't enjoy this dick I'm giving you?"

"Yeah... I do," I moaned.

Now that wasn't a lie. I enjoyed it, but I couldn't say I loved it. However, before I could really get into it, he said, "Fuck... I'm about to cum."

Well ain't this some bullshit. I laid there, watching his face frown up. He took his last thrust and grunted loudly. He was on his fucking way out the door. "Damn, girl," he said as he rolled off me.

I stood and went to the bathroom and cleaned up. When I came back to the bedroom, this muthafucka was getting dressed. "Where are you going?"

"I have to work a double shift, so I have to get back to work."

"You know what? Don't bother coming back, Bashir. You could have told me that earlier, before you brought that whack ass dick in here."

"Whack? You didn't think it was whack when you was bouncing that stale pussy on it."

"Get the fuck out."

He snatched his keys off the dresser and walked his three-minute ass out the door.

K enny

"Did y'all enjoy the night?"

"I did!" Karima yelled.

"Yeah, Dad. We miss you."

"I miss y'all, too."

We were in an Uber, heading back to the condo. I'd taken the kids to MoMaks Backyard Malts and Burgers and they'd had an amazing time. The restaurant was geared towards kids and it was a family environment. My original plan had included Keisha, until she walked in with that nigga she was wasting time with. She didn't know what was about to happen, but I was finna explode on her ass. Had it not been for my kids and that fuck nigga being there, I would have earlier. But she was gonna get this shit as soon as the kids went to bed.

When we arrived, the kids ran to the door and knocked. I was trying to be respectful of her privacy, but she had to know that I had a

39

key to this bitch if I was the one paying for it. By the time I made it to the door, the kids were walking inside, and Keisha was asking them how they enjoyed their night. When I walked through the door, I walked right past her to go take a shower in the guest bathroom. She gave me a weird look, but if she knew like I did, she'd better keep her fucking comments to herself. We'd eaten our food outdoors and I couldn't go to bed smelling like outside, as my mama would say.

When I came out, KJ was standing there waiting to go in. That was perfect. Hopefully, she'd already gotten Karima in the bed. I went to baby girl's bedroom, and sure enough, she was in bed. I kissed her cheek and made my way to the front to find Keisha in the kitchen. "We need to talk."

"Yes, we do. Are you planning to stay here?"

"Yeah."

"Hell no. That's not gon' work, Kenny. You can't stay up in my fucking house."

She looked like she immediately regretted her words, but it was too fucking late. My lip was twitching, and my face was hot as hell. I was the laidback one of the Henderson men, but all hell was about to break loose. "First of all, lower your fucking voice when you talk to me. Secondly, as long as I'm paying the fucking rent and all the other bills in this muthafucka, I will come and go as I please. I've been trying to give you time to get out of your feelings about the shit that happened between us, but you taking the shit overboard. Come sit on the couch."

I walked out of the kitchen and waited for her to join me. When she did, she opened her mouth like she wanted to say something, but I held my hand up, stopping her. "You've been running your mouth for the past two years like I was the only muthafucka that fucked up. So, since we're here, I believe it's time to get some shit out in the open. I was wrong for cheating. But being ignored by your wife is some hurtful shit. After over six months of that shit, I didn't have the wherewithal to turn sex from another woman down. I felt guilty about the shit and I'd promised you I wouldn't do it again. You accepted that apology and we agreed to move on from it... together. Okay, fast forward two months. Who do I see coming out of the precinct one building in China with Reggie's ass at ten at night? You said you were going on a girls' night out with some friends."

Her face was flushed, and she looked pale. That was saying a lot for her chocolate complexion. "I guess because I hadn't said anything, you continued pointing the fucking finger at me like I didn't know what you were doing. I followed y'all to his house in Beaumont. But you know what I fucking did? I blamed myself, thinking that if I hadn't cheated first, then this wouldn't have happened. I tried to show you that I was sorry and tried to make shit up to you, but how could I do that when you were forming a fucking relationship with someone else?"

"Kenny, I'm sorry."

"Man, shut the fuck up with that shit. You laying in the bed next to me at night, saying you can't have sex with me because you don't trust me after what happened the first time, but you was fucking Reggie. My sister's ex-boyfriend and my fucking classmate. And y'all kept that shit up for years. So, if anybody got used, it was me. You stayed with me for my money, so you wouldn't have to find a fucking job. And even after knowing all this shit, I still take care of your ass. Not only did you cheat, but you were taking my money. I'm not a fool by far, Keisha. I have a good heart, but you gon' fucking turn that shit black. I love you and I love my kids. That's the only reasons why you've gotten away with all the shit you did."

The tears were falling from her eyes and she wanted to act all hurt in this bitch, like she hadn't been a conniving whore for years. But I still wanted her. What in the fuck did that say about me? "The icing on the cake was when I asked you to braid my hair and when I asked to use a car that I'm fucking paying for. Who in the fuck do you think you are? Huh? That's a real ass question. 'Cause I wanted to grab you by yo' fucking throat before we left. All the shit I'm doing for you and you got the nerve to tell me what I can and can't do?"

"Kenny, you hurt me. And I wanted to hurt you back."

"Well, mission fucking accomplished. I know I was wrong, but you withheld sex from me, only giving me a taste every now and then, for almost a fucking year. Had we not always fucked like rabbits, that would have been different. But you never wanted to tell me what was going on with you. Just that you didn't feel like it. But when I finally succumbed to temptation, I get fucking crucified. So, tell me who was hurt first? You know how much I love you and that I would do anything for you, but after you kept fucking Reggie, I said to hell with it. You only fucked me when it benefitted you. I fucked different women... yeah. I did that because I didn't wanna catch feelings for nobody but you. However, you had done caught feelings for a nigga that don't give a shit about you. A nigga that used to be my homeboy. But after all that shit, I held onto you because I felt like because of what I did, I deserved that shit."

She dropped her face to her hands as I stood from the couch. I was tired of her bullshit. It may have been best for me to just let her go, because this shit between us was toxic as fuck. "You better put all that money you took from me into good use, because my handouts stop here. You will get child support. That's it. That shit is over two grand a month. If that ain't enough, I suggest you get a fucking job."

I stood to walk to the back room. As soon as I walked off, she said, "Kenny, wait."

I turned to her, feeling disgusted that I had to even speak to her that way. I'd never spoken to any woman as harshly as I had spoken to her. Not even Tasha's triflin' ass. "I don't have any money," she said softly.

When she said that shit, I only got angrier. "So, you mean to tell me that you took almost one hundred thousand from me over the years and you ain't got a penny to your name?"

"No."

"I better get out of here before I fuck you up."

Her eyes widened as I walked to the door. Her saying she didn't have any money left could only mean one thing. She'd tricked off my money to that nigga Reggie. When I got back to Nome, it was gon' be hell to pay. I didn't wanna tell my family what was going on, but I was coming to his ass Henderson style, with my brothers behind me. That shit might have been the nail in our fucking coffin. How could I continue loving a woman that would steal from me? Had she kept it for herself, I wouldn't have called her a thief, because what was mine was hers. But this fuck shit? I'd never hit a woman and I wanted to keep a clean record before I laid her ass out.

As I walked around the complex, I thought about how our marriage went wrong. All she had to do was talk to me. I still didn't know why she wouldn't have sex with me at first. Was she cheating then? Naw. She couldn't have been. She'd just had Karima. While I thought it could have been postpartum, I didn't know for sure. If that was the reason, why in the fuck wouldn't she tell me that shit? I was the man she was supposed to love with all her heart. I loved that woman and did everything I could to keep her happy. She didn't ask for a lot, but I made sure to show her how much I loved and cherished her.

How did we get to this?

After I'd made it around the complex, I went to the door and sat on the ground. Money that I'd worked hard for, she was giving it to another nigga. Naw. That shit wasn't gon' fly. No matter how much I tried to cool off, it wasn't happening. I walked back inside to find her sitting in the same spot, playing on her phone. She was probably texting somebody. Her head snapped up and she looked at me with fear in her eyes. "So, check this out. Y'all not staying in San Antonio. You're moving back either to Nome or Beaumont. My kids are not going to be suffering the way I am because they miss me. If you wanna stay here, you can stay by yourself, because I'll be coming back for my children."

Her tears started up again and I didn't feel a thing. I sat in the chair across from her and asked, "Why wouldn't you have sex with me? I need to know. Were you seeing somebody else, even then? Why?"

"When I went for my six-week checkup, after I had Karima, I was diagnosed with postpartum depression. I wanted to tell you, but I didn't know how to explain it. Instead of being upset with being a mother, I was upset with being a wife. It was like, I didn't feel desirable anymore. No matter how much you complimented me, I couldn't feel it."

"So, why in the fuck you couldn't tell me that then? Do you know we wouldn't have gone through any of the shit we went through? I tried to be there for you. I did most of the housework and took care of KJ when he got out of school. Had him doing homework at the convenience store, all to make things easy on you."

"It's not my fault for getting postpartum!"

"I didn't say it was your fucking fault for being depressed. I said you should have told me! Me! The man that dedicated his entire life to you! I gave you everything I had! You held my heart and soul in your hands! There was nothing I wouldn't do for you. Yet you ridiculed me in front of my family, like all this shit was on me. And I let you do that, even though I knew you were fucking Reggie. I let you tear me down and I kept your secret, because I felt like it was my fault that you cheated. That ship has sailed, Keisha. They about to know the truth. And you better hope Tiffany don't kill yo' ass."

As I stood to my feet, my phone started to ring. I didn't recognize the number, so I answered cautiously. "Hello?"

"Kenny, this is Tasha."

"Great. My other baby mama. What the fuck *you* want?"

She was quiet as hell, probably trying to figure out if she had the right number. She finally got out, "I wanted to know if I could start my every two weekends with Kendrick next weekend. I finally got my shit together and I have a nice place that I feel comfortable with him staying in. I live in Dayton now, so I'm not that far."

"Yeah. I'll hit you back tomorrow so we can get this in writing."

"Oh... okay."

I ended the call and turned to see KJ standing in the hallway watching us. "Is everything okay? I heard yelling."

"It's fine, man. Go back to your room. I'll be in there in a little bit."

He looked at Keisha, I'm sure seeing her tears, then turned to go to his room. He hesitated, then turned back to us. "Mama, everything okay?" he asked her while glancing at me.

"Yeah, baby. Everything's okay."

He nodded, then walked away. Keisha looked at me and I could still see the fear in her eyes. "Kendrall... Kenny, I'm sorry. Seeing you like this made me realize just how wrong I am for everything. This isn't you, but it's who I've forced you to become. I'll move back so you and the kids can see one another more often."

She stood from her seat and walked a little closer to me. "If you still want me to, I'll braid your hair."

"Naw. I'll get Tiffany to do it when I get back. I don't want you touching me."

I walked off to the room I was gonna share with my son for the night. When I walked in, he was lying on his back, staring at the ceiling. Before I could say a word to him, my phone rang again. When I saw it was my mama, I answered, "Hello?"

"Hey, baby. Kendrick is a little whiny, so I wanted him to hear your voice."

"Okay."

"Okay. You're on speaker."

"Hey, lil man. It's your dad. What's the matter?"

"Da-Da."

That brought a smile to my face. He rarely called me anything. He was always crying. "Kenny, he's smiling."

"I am, too."

"How are my other grandbabies?"

"They're fine, Ma. KJ is right here next to me."

"Oh! Let me talk to my baby."

I handed the phone to him as he sat there staring at me. While he and Mama talked, I sat and thought about how I went off on Keisha. She deserved every word. *Why did I feel so bad about it, though?*

45

Taking off my shirt, I got in bed as KJ talked and laughed with Mama and his little brother. Instead of focusing on how I talked to Keisha, I decided to focus on the meeting I was gonna call with my brothers, including Ryder. He's proved that he has always had our back, but I needed to talk to them since Reggie was a fucking cop. I didn't want to kill him, but I did want to fuck him up and scare him shitless. Make him wanna regret ever fucking with me or anyone in my family. Ever since he'd fucked over Tiff, I've had little to say to his bitch ass. But now? I was gon' have plenty to talk about.

When KJ got off the phone with Mama, he handed the phone to me. She'd hung up, so I assumed she didn't have anything more to talk to me about. As we got comfortable in his queen-sized bed, he looked at me and asked, "Do you hate Mama?"

"Not at all, son. I'm just angry about some things. Don't worry yourself with what's going on with us. We gon' work it out. Okay?"

"Yes sir. Can I ask one more question before I go to sleep?"

"Yeah."

"Are we moving back to Nome?"

"I don't know about Nome, but y'all will be moving closer to where I can see y'all more often."

He held his fist up and I gave him a pound, then pushed his head. "Get some rest."

"Goodnight, Dad."

"Goodnight."

Within minutes, he was snoring. Now it was my turn to stare at the ceiling. Grabbing my phone, I sent a group message to WJ, Jasper, Storm, and Ryder. *Can we all meet Monday morning at about eight? I got some shit I need to get off my chest and I'm gon' need backup.*

I chose eight, because Ryder didn't usually have to get to his shop until ten. Same with Storm and Jasper. WJ came and went as he pleased. One by one, they all responded their confirmations. But of course, not to disappoint, Storm had to call. "Hello?"

"What the fuck happened?"

"If I could talk about it now, Storm, I wouldn't have texted. I won't be back in town until late tomorrow night."

"A'ight. Well, just answer this shit. Is it about Keisha or directly related to her? Because my ears done got ahold to some shit that I ain't feeling at all."

"Hell yeah."

"A'ight. I'm ready for war my nigga. Just say the word. I never liked that grimy muthafucka."

I knew he was talking about Reggie. It felt good to hear somebody have my back and I knew the rest of my family would fall in line as well.

❧ 6 ❧

K eisha

"HEY, GIRL. I WAS CALLING TO CHECK ON YOU. I AIN'T HEARD from your ass all day."

"I've been in bed pretty much the whole day. I broke up with Bashir yesterday, and not long after, Kenny tore me a new asshole. He knew the entire time about my affair. The incident he described was only my second time sleeping with Reggie."

"Oh shit! What made him bring it up?"

"I believe he snapped. He said he'd been mild, trying to give me time to get over my disappointments and hurt, but he's had enough. I'd told him he couldn't stay at my fucking house. That was when he lost it."

"Damn it, Keisha! What did we talk about?"

"I know. The minute I said it, I wanted to jump through time to grab it back. Cass, I've never seen Kenny look the way he did last night. It scared the shit out of me. The way he spoke to me broke me down to my core. I didn't sleep a wink last night. Plus... he demanded that I move closer so he can see the kids more often."

"Shit! He finally found his muthafucking balls. Ain't no way I would have let you talk to me the way you talked to him. He took all that shit like a G while knowing all that shit. Man, that's love, for real. You woulda got fucked up messing with me. You should've sucked his dick to apologize."

I rolled my eyes. "I'd declined to braid his hair earlier that day by text. So, I offered to do it last night and he told me he didn't want me touching him."

"Fuck. He really mad at yo' ass. I promise he wouldn't have minded you touching his dick, though."

"Shut up, Cass."

"I bet you didn't tell Kenny to shut up last night."

I rolled my eyes while she laughed. Ain't shit was funny. Kenny had left a little over three hours ago and Karima had cried for at least an hour after he left. When he kissed them bye, I just knew he would ignore me, but he even told me bye. He didn't touch me, though. I hated the level I'd caused him to stoop to. I'd taken his kindness for weakness. That cliché was real last night. Kenny had never spoken to me that way and I'd never witnessed him speaking that way to anyone else, either. He was angry, and my admission about the money had really hurt him.

I was so bitter at the time. I'd been taking money, stashing it in a personal account for years. I'd take a couple hundred dollars at a time, probably once a week, sometimes twice. That money was supposed to be a cushion for if I ever got the nerve to leave him. Somehow, I let Reggie finesse me out of all that money. I wasn't taking the money with the intent to give it to Reggie. It was supposed to be for me and my children. I was such a fool. One time he'd said his mama couldn't have a surgery until she met her deductible, so she had to come up with five grand. I felt bad for him and gave him the money. After that, he always needed money for something. He'd never come out and ask, but he never turned the money down, either.

I stood from the bed and went to check on Karima. Only hours after Kenny left, her fever came back. My kids were depressed without their dad. Everything he said... he was right. "Hellooooo! Is anybody on the phone?"

"I'm still here, Cass."

"So, what are you gonna do?"

"Whatever the fuck he tell me to do if I don't wanna be out on the streets."

"Bitch, you better. I wish I could have been a fly on the fucking wall. I know you were probably in your feelings, but you brought that shit on yourself."

I huffed loudly. "Are you my friend or Kenny's? 'Cause right now, I can't tell."

"Shit, right now I don't know whose friend I am. My friend Keisha used to be a loyal, loving, and honest woman. Somehow, you became this bitter, evil liar when it concerned the man you were supposed to love through the good and bad times. I wouldn't be your friend if I didn't give you the real. You know that."

"I do. That's why I keep yo' ass around. You tried to warn me about sleeping with Reggie after I first told you about it. I love you, Cass."

"I love you, too."

A small cry escaped me as I balled up in the fetal position in my bed, realizing that all my bullshit had caught up with me. "Keisha don't cry. How's Karima?"

"Her fever came back. Kenny's only been gone for three hours and they've fallen back into their depressive states."

"Why don't you tell them y'all are moving back, so they could see their dad more?"

"I'm gonna go tell her now. I have to give her some medicine. I'll call you back."

"No need. I'm on my way there with some boxes to help you start packing."

"Thanks, Cass."

I ended the call and went to the kitchen to get Karima's medicine, then made my way to her room. While I wanted to sulk and just be to myself, I still had to be a mother. When I walked in her room, she was sitting on side of her bed. "What's the matter, baby?" I asked as I sat beside her with her medicine.

"I miss, Daddy," she responded, then burst into tears.

My heart sank to my feet. I pulled her to my lap and held her in my arms. "I'm so sorry, baby. But guess what?" I asked as I wiped her tears.

"What?"

"We're moving back close to your daddy. Probably by next month. Let me call him and see if it can be sooner. Okay?"

"Okay, Mommy. I love you," she said as she hugged my neck.

Holding the tears inside was hard, but I didn't want my baby to see me cry. I walked out her room and let the tears escape me. All this time, I thought they would get better. KJ had been in his room since Kenny left. Whoever said kids were resilient and adjusted to change quickly were liars. My babies had only worsened. With all my hang-ups, I was a good mother. I took care of my children, and when they hurt, it hurt me, too.

I went to my bedroom and grabbed my phone to call Kenny. He answered on the first ring. "The kids okay?"

My heart sank, because I realized I only called him about the kids if something was wrong. I rarely called him to tell him the good things they may had done. "The kids are fine."

"So, what'chu calling me for, Keisha?"

"I wanted to ask if the kids and I could move back sooner and stay in Nome until I can find a job and another place."

He was quiet as hell. "I'm not leaving my house and I don't know if I want you sleeping under the same roof as me. I have another son to raise, also. I'm not uprooting him from his home to appease you. Give me time to think about it."

He ended the call. This Kenny I'd awakened scared the hell out of me. Now that everything was out in the open, I felt vulnerable, broken, and in despair. *The same way Kenny had been feeling for years.* At the thought of that, I broke down. Why couldn't I see the error of my ways sooner? As I sat there crying, feeling sorry for how I treated Kenny, the doorbell rang. Going to it, I expected it to be Cass, so I just opened it without looking through the peep hole. It was Bashir. "I just wanted to come back and apologize. I was out of character. Whether you accept it or not, I had to come back and at least try to make it right."

"I apologize, too."

"Can I come in?"

"I don't think that's a good idea. We should just cut our losses."

He grabbed my hand and held it between his and smiled, then pulled me to him. After hugging me tightly, he said, "I hope that we can remain friends... the way we started."

"Maybe so. Thanks for being a great friend."

He kissed my forehead and left just as Cass was walking up. She glanced at him as he said, "What's up, Cass?"

"Hey," she said dismissively.

She never really liked Bashir. She'd always been rooting for me and Kenny to work things out. I didn't talk to her for a week because of that. "What in the fuck did he want? I thought y'all broke up yesterday?"

"We did, but he came back to apologize for some shit he said, and I apologized for what I said to provoke him."

"What the hell did you say?"

"I called his dick whack."

"What the fuck? Man, you crazy."

"I know."

Truth was, I was in my feelings that he wasn't Kenny and that I would probably never find a man that was as good to me as he was. I was angry with myself for turning a loyal, selfless man into a huge man-whore. One that was willing to have unprotected sex with various women. The first year of our relationship, he'd refused sex if he didn't have a condom. My behavior corrupted him. I had become the woman that other women that were looking for a good man despised. But I had no choice now but to prove to Kenny that I could be the woman he once fell in love with. I didn't think he wanted me back at this point, but if we could at least be friends, then I'd be satisfied.

As I walked through the house, heading back to my room, Cass grabbed my hand. "Keisha, don't do that. I can see the depression looming. Again, you brought this shit on yourself. Put your granny panties on, suck that shit up, and do what you can to fix it."

I took a deep breath. "Shit, you right. Hol' on."

I grabbed my phone and called Kenny back and put the phone on speaker. "What Keisha?" he answered.

"I'm having my things put in storage and the kids and I are coming next week. I'll send the info to you to get them back in school. I'm going to prove to you that I can be the woman you love. I know you still love me, Kenny. I love you, too, and I'm sorry for everything. Even if we never get back together, I want us to eventually have a good relationship. I know I have to pay for what I did, and I'm gonna work hard to do that."

He was quiet for a second, then he answered, "The kids can stay with me. But I need more time to think about where you gon' stay. Keisha, I'm not just angry. This shit has been building for years. So just like you seemed to be disgusted with me and my actions, I'm disgusted with you. Don't try to force my hand about this. Now, don't call me no more. I'll call you."

He ended the call as I stared at Cass. "Naw, suck that shit up. You can't make demands. So, be okay with sleeping in your car if you have to. And you may have to."

"I'm okay with that, Cass. I'm gon' sleep right there in his driveway. One thing I know about Kenny is that he's soft-hearted. I'm gonna use that to my advantage. I do love him. You know that."

"I know. I just hope he can forgive you. I can hear the anger in his voice."

"Me too, Cass. Me too."

7

K enny

"So, you mean to tell me, you went without sex for almost ten fucking months while she was laying next to you?"

"Yep. Almost a year, Jasper."

"That's why yo' ass would get so defensive when I was talking to you about cheating and how perfect she was. She was fucking up from the beginning. That's admirable of you, brother."

"Fuck that. That shit was stupid. Ain't no way I would have let her bad mouth me to my family and let everybody think she was perfect. I would have blasted her ass a long time ago. When that nigga, Sisco, said people were talking about Reggie fucking her, I was ready to knock that nigga out. But I ain't ever caught Sisco talking out the side of his neck. So, I knew that shit was reputable coming from his ass." Storm said.

I rolled my eyes as Ryder and Jasper laughed and nodded in

agreement with Storm. All my brothers were there and even Red, Zayson, and Legend had met us at Jasper's barber shop. I'd gotten close to them through my brothers. They were all like brothers to us, too. They were gonna be at Red's to practice today anyway. I was almost sure that Storm had told them to come. I'd told them everything that had gone down between me and Keisha from the time she had Karima until Saturday night, and they were shocked to say the least. "That bitch would have been out the door," WJ said.

Everyone's eyebrows went up, including mine. That nigga had nerve, especially when his wife had cheated on him. They were working things out in their marriage and I never once heard him call her a bitch, so he wasn't about to get away with calling Keisha one. "Yo, WJ. What she did was triflin' as hell, but you not finna disrespect her by calling her a bitch. If anybody gon' do that, it's gon' be me. So, if I ain't done it, I don't know what makes you think it would be okay for you to do it. She's still the mother of my children and I still love her. This meeting ain't about getting at her. It's about getting at Reggie's punk ass."

"Well, count me out. You not saying shit about all that to her for all those years... that's what you get. Get a backbone, Kenny," he said, shaking his head.

WJ walked out the barbershop and I was trying to figure out what was up his ass early this morning already. Grouchy ass. "Fuck his miserable ass," Storm said.

"This the shit I wanna know, Kenny," Jasper started. "She was fucking with that nigga while he was with Tiff?"

I frowned, because I never thought about that shit. Only that he was Tiffany's ex. Everybody was frowning. "Either that or before he started fucking with Tiff. He and Tiff only messed around for a year or so, and that was when Karima was two or three. So, I guess so. But it seems like he was fucking Keisha first. Whatever the fuck happened, she knew about him and Tiff."

"That's fucked up. Reggie 'bout to feel some shit. He pursued Tiff when he knew he was fucking your wife?" Legend said.

"Yeah, I suppose so."

"Man, Kenny, don't ever keep no shit like this to yourself. You know we got yo' back," Jasper said.

I nodded, as I thought about Keisha calling me twice after I left yesterday. She was only hurting because I told her of what all I knew. I didn't have time for the shit. I'd gotten home last night and had called Tasha's ass back. She would be getting Kendrick this coming weekend. I loved my son, but I could use a break. He didn't seem to be too whiny last night, but we would see how the rest of the week went. "So, what we gon' do about that muthafucka?" Red asked.

"I say we catch his ass wit' his pants down. The muthafucka always got hoe activities going on at his house. He live by Kortlynn's mama. So, whenever we go over there and he off, he always got company," Zay said.

"Hell yeah. We oughta beat his ass with his own club," Storm said standing to his feet, grabbing the bat from the corner.

He started swinging and we all started laughing, I needed this bonding shit. It was hard carrying all the shit by myself. "Okay, I say we watch his ass for a while before we do anything. Zay, you keep an eye on his ass in Beaumont and China, and y'all Nome niggas got this area covered. Me and Legend can watch his ass if he ever roll to Liberty," Ryder said.

We all shook hands and hugged one another. "We'll come up with a solid plan when we know his comings and goings. In the meantime, I'm going holla at WJ's bitch ass," Jasper added as we all laughed.

Ryder headed out to get to Baytown for his ten o'clock appointment and everyone else filed out as well while I sat quietly for a moment. Jasper sat next to me and said, "I can't believe all this shit man. I thought you were following Daddy's footsteps, but it's a lot deeper than I thought."

"I love Keisha. I really do, even after all this bullshit. I'm just so angry and I don't know if I could ever trust her again. My efforts to get her back have been put on pause... possibly indefinitely."

"No one would blame you. I hate that we all judged you without knowing the whole story."

"I didn't give y'all much of choice because I wanted to protect Keisha from y'all," I said, then chuckled. "But Saturday, I knew that I had to let all that shit go. My kids are suffering. She called yesterday, still apologizing and wanting to move back sooner."

His eyebrows rose. "What did you say?"

"I told her my kids could stay here, but I didn't know about her. I'm still pissed about her giving that muthafucka my money, man. It's bad enough she was giving him my pussy, not to mention her heart. All that shit was supposed to be mine. But since I cheated first..." I shrugged my shoulders as Jasper pat my back.

"Don't beat yo'self up, bruh. I got'chu. We all got'chu. You know we don't give a fuck about no fucking police. We're Hendersons. And that Henderson done come out of yo' ass. When you walked through the door, I was like ooohh shit."

I chuckled. "Thanks, Jasper."

"Man, you ain't gotta thank me. But I do have something to tell you. Kendrick ain't hardly whined while you were gone. You know what I think?"

"What?" I asked, my interest piqued.

"He's feeling your misery. He knows you aren't happy. If you let all that shit go and truly be happy with you and him, I think things will change. I know you're angry right now, but watch what I'm telling you."

"You might be right. Well, I gotta get to the convenience store. I'm meeting with your wife and a contractor about making the store a truck stop."

"Oh, that's what's up."

"Yeah. Plus, Shylou done had enough. I'm about to go talk to him, too."

Jasper shook my hand and said, "Well, good luck with everything, bruh."

"Thanks."

I left out the shop and headed to the store, my mind full of shit I could do to Reggie's conniving, backstabbing ass. If Keisha was fucking him while he was with Tiffany, I didn't know how I would react to that. Not only had she betrayed me, but my sister, too? Taking a deep breath, I parked and walked in the store to see Chasity, Jasper's wife, waiting with the contractor. After looking at the time, I realized I was ten minutes late. *Oh well.* Shylou was also waiting with them, keeping them company. When I walked through the door, the contractor said, "And there he is."

He walked over to me and shook my hand, then I hugged Chasity. After shaking Shylou's hand, I suggested that we get started with our meeting so we could get done.

❦

THE MEETINGS HAD GONE WELL, AND SHYLOU WAS ONLY ASKING for two hundred fifty grand to buy him out. I didn't know how I would handle spending all this money right now and take care of my children, but I had to make it work. I didn't want to be partnered with someone I didn't know. When I got to my mama's house, I was a little stressed. I sat in the truck and tried to calm down a bit. Taking deep breaths, I could feel the nerves dissipating. Then there was a knock on my window that scared the shit out of me. I opened the door, "Storm, you scared the shit outta me."

"I know. That's why I did it. You done for the day?"

"Yeah. I was coming to get Kendrick, so I could head home."

"Yeah. I came to get Tweedledee and Tweedledum and their friend Alice."

I chuckled at Storm's reference of his three girls. "Where's baby boy?"

"He's with Aspen. She can still get shit done with him at home. Plus, she's breastfeeding."

"Oh okay."

We both headed inside to get our children as my phone rang.

59

That shit had been ringing off the hook. I was so sick of the robocalls and solicitors. I looked at it to see Keisha's phone number. I rolled my eyes and ignored the call. I told her that I would call her when I made a decision. When we got to the door and I could hear the kids screaming and yelling. "That has to be the twins, acting a fool like that."

"You know it is. They always raising hell," Storm said as we walked in.

Bali was lying on top of Kendrick while he screamed with laughter. She was tickling him. I'd never heard him laugh that way before and it brought a smile to my face. Storm stood there, shaking his head as he smiled at the kids. They continued playing until Noni yelled, "Da-dy!"

Bali hopped off Kendrick and ran to Storm along with Noni and their youngest sister Maui. They looked like triplets instead of twins. When they did, Kendrick stood to his feet and looked at me like he wanted to run to me like they did Storm. So, I smiled and stretched out my arms. He smiled big and ran to me. I just knew tears were going to fall down my face. After spinning around with him, I went to hug and kiss my mama. "Thanks for watching him, Ma. I don't think I'll be doing anything significant where he can't be with me."

"Okay, baby. I can watch him anytime. Umm... Keisha called me."

My anger was coming back, so I put Kendrick down as Storm walked closer to us. "For what?" I asked.

"She wanted to apologize for everything. I just said okay, but I didn't have the slightest clue what she was talking about."

"Aww shit," Storm said.

"She assumed I'd told you. She cheated on me with Reggie. He was her side nigga for years. It started after my first affair. So, she's probably apologizing for dragging my name through the mud, making it seem like she was a saint."

My mama had covered her mouth. I refused to go through the whole story. I didn't have it in me. It was bad enough I had to tell it to the fellas today. "I knew it had to be something. Out of all my children, you are the most mild-mannered and sweetest. You aren't a selfish cheater. That wasn't who you were. It was so out of character for you. I knew there had to be more to this than what I knew, but I didn't want to keep asking questions. So, I assumed she thought you'd told me about it."

"I suppose so. She just found out that I knew about it this past weekend."

"Kenny... baby come here. My soft-hearted child."

Storm rolled his eyes as Mama hugged me tightly. I smiled at him and said, "I knew I was your favorite."

"My middle baby. Y'all are all my favorites."

"She only said that so you wouldn't feel bad," I said to Storm.

"Whatever nigga," he said then pushed me in the head.

He thought because he was a whole five inches taller than me, he could push me around. I felt someone wrap their arms around my legs and it was Kendrick. I picked him up and hugged him tightly. I think Jasper was right about what he'd said. He wrapped his arms around my neck and laid on my shoulder. They hadn't had a nap yet, so I knew he was tired. "You wanna eat, lil man?"

Mama had spaghetti fixed for them, so I sat at the table with him and fed him the spaghetti while the twins made a complete mess in their highchairs trying to feed themselves. Storm was fussing as usual, but those girls had him wrapped around their fingers. Once I finished feeding him, we headed home. He was asleep before we got there. After going inside, I laid him in my bed, then left the room to call Keisha. Before the phone could barely ring, she answered, "Hello?"

"Why did you call my mama with that bullshit?"

"I thought you told her. You said everyone was about to know about my fuckups. I just wanted to apologize."

"You don't call nobody in my family but me. You hear me?"

"I'm sorry."

"My kids can stay, Keisha, but I can't deal wit'chu."

"Where am I supposed to go, Kenny?"

"I don't know. Call Reggie."

I could hear her crying, but I refused to acknowledge her tears. "I'm driving down Friday. I'll bring the kids to your house. We should be there by eight or nine that night."

"Okay."

"Kenny?"

"Yeah?"

"You think you'll ever be able to forgive me?"

"I don't know, Keisha. I feel like if I hadn't told you that I knew everything except the last part you told me, you would still be treating me like shit. That's the part that I'm having a hard time understanding. Why treat me like I'm shit? We're already divorced and have been for almost two years. There was no point in treating me like I don't matter. But that's over with and I'm just trying to get past it. Once I can stop rehashing all the details and handle some last business, I can be totally done with it and begin healing from it."

"I won't bring it up again, that's for sure. We'll be there Friday and I'll drop the kids to you. I'll let them call when they get out of school."

"Okay."

I ended the call and rubbed my hand down my face as I stood to go to the kitchen. I'd taken out some chicken to bake. Once that was done, I could relax. But I knew that thoughts of Keisha not having anywhere to go was gonna drive me insane.

8

K eisha

"Kenny, we're about ten minutes away."

"Okay. The gate is open."

When I ended the call, I woke up KJ and Karima. They'd both fallen asleep on the five-hour drive. We were also pulling a trailer from U-Haul with all their things in it, along with all our clothes. Kenny always made sure we wanted for nothing, so our clothes alone took up over half of the six by twelve foot trailer. The kids were excitedly putting on their shoes. I was excited for them, too, but not knowing where I was gonna go from here was scary. Especially since everyone I knew was in San Antonio. Everyone I knew or was friends with here, were connected to Kenny.

When I turned in the driveway, Karima screamed in excitement. I smiled at her, then looked at the house. It looked the exact same way as when we left. I got out of the car and stretched as Kenny came outside. The kids ran to him and hugged him tightly as his little boy peered at us through the storm door. Karima ran to him. When she got inside, she picked him up and swung him around as he laughed. He looked just like Kenny. Kenny walked over to me and asked, "How was the drive?"

"It was okay."

"Let me back this trailer in, so we can unpack all this tomorrow."

"My things are in there, too. I need to turn it in by tomorrow evening before U-Haul closes."

"Give me a minute."

I watched him back the trailer close to the door, then he got out of the car and said, "Come inside."

When I walked in, I saw a little suitcase by the door. Kendrick must have been going to be with his mother. The kids ran to their rooms with Kendrick hanging on for dear life as I nervously sat on the couch across from Kenny. This past week had been rough. I hadn't talked to him since Monday night and I didn't know what he was about to say now. He stood from his seat and sat next to me. "You can stay here tonight. We'll worry about the other days when they get here. You know where the guestrooms are upstairs. One of them is now Kendrick's room."

I quickly hugged him and whispered, "Thank you so much, Kenny. I promise to stay out of your way. You won't know I'm here."

When I let him go, he was completely red in the face. I hadn't hugged him in a long time. "I'm sorry. I'm just happy that you had a change of heart."

He nodded as he stood and went to the kitchen. "Have y'all eaten?"

"We ate before we left San Antonio, but they're probably hungry again. They were too excited to stop."

I chuckled softly. I was glad to be here, too. Kenny's mood had changed drastically since Monday evening. He seemed like the old Kenny. Maybe when he went off on my ass last weekend, he was releasing everything he'd been holding inside for years. I didn't know what he'd cooked, but my stomach was growling. It smelled delicious. When the kids came downstairs, Kenny grabbed Kendrick and put him in his highchair, then sat plates of food in front of KJ and Karima. "You wanna eat, Keisha?"

I stood from the couch and gave him a soft smile. "Please?"

He motioned with his head for me to come over. For some reason, I felt nervous. When I got to him, I saw that he'd smothered some deer meat. Something I knew nothing about until I met him almost seventeen years ago. "It smells good, Kenny."

"Thank you."

He fixed me a plate of rice and gravy, green beans, and meat. The kids were quiet and even Kendrick was sitting there licking his fingers. I took the plate from him and said, "Thank you so much."

He nodded, then fixed his plate. He joined us at the table and fed Kendrick some green beans as the doorbell rang. A slight frown made its way to his face, so I assumed that was Tasha's bitch-ass. That kick she got to her face was still fresh in my memory. I hated her ass, because she didn't know how to keep Kenny's infidelities discreet. She wanted the world to know. Maybe it was best that everyone knew. It changed the both of us. Kenny went to the door and opened it. Tasha stood there with a smile on her face until she saw me. She walked in and went straight to Kendrick. "Hey, baby!"

She hugged him tightly as he looked at her like she was crazy. He peeped over at Kenny, like he was trying to figure out who she was. "Baby boy, it's me! Mommy!"

"Ma-ma," Kendrick got out.

"Yes! You remember me!"

She seemed extra hyped, like she was high or something. Kenny had a frown on his face as she talked to Kendrick. Kendrick finally smiled at her. KJ and Karima kept glancing at her, too, like they thought she was off. She took Kendrick from his highchair, so Kenny walked them to the door. When they got there, I saw him take out his phone and turn the light on to look into her eyes. I guess he was checking to see if her pupils were dilated. Everything must have been okay, so he kissed Kendrick's head and told her to be careful and to call when they made it to Dayton.

Dayton was only about thirty minutes away. Kenny walked the two of them out as the three of us kept eating in silence. I supposed no one wanted to say anything to offend me. Seeing Tasha didn't offend me. I just didn't like her as a person. But who was I to even dislike anybody? When Kenny came back inside, he said, "So, are y'all glad to be back?"

"Beyond! I'm ready to go roll all over the cow pasture," KJ said excitedly.

Kenny chuckled as I smiled at him. But when he looked at me, I didn't know if I liked what I saw in his eyes. Something was going on and I was almost sure I would find out why he was being so nice to me before long. We continued enjoying our meal and, for the first time in a long time, we felt like a family. When we were done, I volunteered to clean the kitchen and Kenny followed the kids to their rooms. I knew they were tired. They'd been awake since early this morning. Their teachers had given them going away parties at school. After all the adrenaline that had been pumping through their bodies all day, they were probably gonna crash.

By the time I finished cleaning the kitchen and had taken a shower, there was a knock on the bedroom door. I opened it to find Kenny standing there. The look on his face was serious. He walked by me and sat on the bed. "Close the door," he said somewhat forcefully.

I didn't know what to think, but I did as he requested, then sat on the bed as well. Not being able to look into his eyes, I trained my gaze on the floor. He lifted my head by putting his fingers under my chin. "This is what I need from you. Tomorrow, Reggie will be patrolling the area. I need for him to see you back in town and you will talk him into letting you go to his house later that night."

What? I was at a loss for words. My lips slightly parted and I realized he was using me to exact revenge on Reggie. I closed my eyes, not believing what I heard. "Is this why you were being so nice to me?"

"I need to be able to see what you're doing. The old saying, keep your friends close but your enemies closer... I need you in my fucking shadow."

I lowered my head, wishing this was just a horrible nightmare I was having... that I was actually back in San Antonio. Looking back at him, I tried to plead with my eyes, but Kenny might as well had been blind. "Kenny, where will he be?"

"I'll call you when he gets to Storm's shop. When I call, you need to go up there, so he'll know you're in town. I'm sure you still have his number, so you can call him later and set something up. Don't look at me like this shit is beneath you. Especially when you took my fucking money and gave it to that muthafucka. You're trifling, conniving, a thief and a liar. Why would I trust you?"

After that, he left the room. I laid back in the bed and reasoned that I owed him more. So, when I saw Reggie, I would be convincing as hell. I had no idea what Kenny had planned for his ass after I went to his house, but I almost didn't want to know. Before I could get under the covers, my cell phone rang. It was my day one. "Hey, Cass."

"Hey. Why you sound like that? I was calling to see if you had made it to Nome."

"Yeah, I'm here. Kenny is allowing me to stay with him because he needs to keep his enemies closer. He said he wanted me to be in his fucking shadow. Cass, he was being so nice to me. I should have known it was put on. He wants me to set Reggie up. I don't know what he's planning, but it can't be good."

As Cass talked, practically having a fit, Kenny swung the door open and jerked the phone from my ear. "See? You can't be trusted. Why would tell that kind of shit to anybody?"

"It was just Cass, Kenny. You know Cass would never betray either one of us."

"That's your friend and there's no telling what kind of lies you've probably fed her."

"She knows the truth Kenny... all of it."

"Figures. She knew before the person who needed to know."

He threw my phone to the bed and slammed the door. Seeing that he'd either ended the call or Cass had hung up, I texted her and said, *I'll talk to you tomorrow.*

Lying in the bed, I pulled the covers over my head and cried myself to sleep.

❧

WHEN I WOKE UP, IT WAS STILL DARK OUTSIDE. KENNY TENDED to wake up early, so I decided to start breakfast. It was only five in the morning, but he was usually up by six. I used to do this every day, serving my family with love, devotion, and loyalty. Back before I lost my damn mind. Well, before we both lost our minds. I was so afraid to tell Kenny about my diagnosis and I have no idea why. He was always so understanding, loving, and comforting. If there was some way I could get his money back, I'd get back every penny.

As I moved around the kitchen, I realized nothing had changed. Everything was still in the same places I'd arranged them in. Had Kenny even been living? I wanted to call Chrissy so badly. Chrissy was his sister right above him in age. She and I had been close until I left. She called me occasionally, along with Tiffany, but I rarely answered or called back. Taking a deep breath, I began mixing ingredients to make pancakes. They deserved the best breakfast I could make them today. There were some deer sausage patties in the fridge, along with bacon. Everything I could cook, I cooked it.

As I finished up the pancakes, I could hear someone coming down the stairs. It was six-thirty. I quickly started the Keurig and poured a glass of orange juice and brought it to the table for Kenny. I loaded his plate with pancakes, biscuits, deer meat, bacon, eggs, sautéed potatoes and grits. When I sat it on the table, I turned and

ran right into him. He grabbed my shoulders and held me steady. "I...
I apologize. Good morning, Kenny. Your breakfast is ready."

I sidestepped him, because I didn't want to look in a face that
hated me. He stood there, staring at the food as I brought more
biscuits and pancakes to the table. After bringing the kids' food to the
table as well, I went upstairs to wake them up. While they were
brushing their teeth, I hurried back downstairs to see if Kenny
needed anything. He was gone. His plate of food was still sitting
there. I picked up my heart off the floor and went to get the syrup and
jelly. I had to do my best to stay positive. Maybe he just went outside
for a moment. That hope was soon shattered when I heard his truck
start.

I picked up his plate and brought it to the stove. Once I wrapped
it in foil, the kids had come downstairs to eat, but I'd lost my appetite.
I didn't feel like eating anymore, because my soul was hurt. While I'd
been saying it was all my fault, I knew we were both to blame for our
failed marriage, infidelities, and betrayal, but my lies and conde-
scending behavior towards him only added insult to injury. As I laid
there on the couch, staring off into space, the back door opened. I sat
up to see Kenny was back. I didn't know where he had gone so
quickly, but my heart ascended to its proper place when I saw him.
He went to the table and looked around, then looked at me. I quickly
stood from the couch. "I'm sorry, I thought you didn't want it."

"I went to bring Tiff some mail that was in my post office box. I
did it now before I forgot."

I nodded, then went to the stove and got his plate. When I sat it
on the table, he said, "Thank you. This looks good."

"Thank you."

I hurriedly fixed me a plate just so I could sit near him for a
while. As I did, I listened to him and the kids chatter about going
back to their old schools and reuniting with their old friends. We both
reached for the syrup at the same time and our hands touched. We
both withdrew our hand and I smiled softly at him. He returned it,
then grabbed the jelly instead. I didn't know what to make of him.

One minute he was nice to me, then the next he was cursing me out and saying he didn't trust me. As the kids finished up, he said, "Y'all go get dressed. We need to go see everybody! Then we'll come back and get your things organized."

The kids quickly left the table with smiles on their faces. Kenny then turned to me. "I would rather you not come yet. Honestly, I don't really know how I feel about you being here, which is why it seems I'm all over the place. Tiffany doesn't know anything, unless Ryder told her. I talked to my brothers and they know everything. I was tired of carrying it. Plus, when I left San Antonio, I was on some other shit. They've been really supportive, and it's helped me a lot. So, chill out here and I'll let you know when Reggie will be at the shop."

"Okay. I understand."

He gently glided his hand down the side of my face. "Why couldn't we have just talked, Keisha?"

I closed my eyes as I swallowed back the tears. "I don't know. We're both stubborn that way, I guess. I was scared to death to tell you how I was feeling, though... about the depression. I'm so sorry. I know you're probably tired of hearing it, but I am. For the record, I didn't take the money to give it to Reggie. I took the money to be able to find somewhere else to live and start a new life with my kids. I'd been planning to leave. Tasha was just too much to handle, because she was carrying your baby. That money was for me and your kids. However, I never thought you would take care of us the way you have been. Thank you, Kenny. Despite the infidelity, you've always been a great dad, amazing provider, and you were a great husband until then. But I realize how my silence pushed you away."

"So, you didn't take my money and give it directly to him?"

"No. I promise that wasn't how it happened. I don't know how I let him talk me out of all that money. He's slick, that's for sure."

"That's just gonna make tonight even sweeter. Can I ask you a question?"

"Yeah. Anything."

"Did you go after him... did you approach him first?"

"No. Reggie had been flirting with me since before Karima was born. I didn't tell you, because I didn't want any trouble or confusion. When he approached me after you'd cheated, I fell. Oh! And he knew that you'd cheated. How would he have known that if I didn't tell him?"

My eyebrows rose as he kissed my forehead and stood from the table. "Nome is small. We all went to school together, so there's no telling. Shardae probably told him."

I could tell Kenny was thinking hard. He was staring off into space and was pulling on his beard. He tended to do that when he was in deep thought or nervous about something. "What are you thinking, Kenny?"

He glanced at me. "I think we were both probably setup. Before Karima was born, Reggie and I were cool, so he knew I was on sexual restriction the last two months of your pregnancy and of course, the six weeks after. He also knew that I wasn't getting any after that. I'ma kill that son of a bitch."

When he used to get angry before, I used to hold him until he'd calmed down. I didn't know what else to do but that. I held him tightly until I felt his heart rate kind of slow down a bit. When I looked up at him, he was staring at me. I held his gaze as I swallowed hard. We had help from outside forces in destroying our union. They caught us at a time when we were most vulnerable, and they capitalized on the shit. We were still staring at each other, so I let him go. "I'm sorry. That was the only thing I knew to do to try to calm you down."

"Surprisingly, it still calmed me, Keisha. But Reggie gon' fucking pay. WJ used to tell me all the time to watch that nigga because he seemed shady. I wish I would've listened."

The kids came running down the stairs before we could talk any further about what we suspected. I didn't know Shardae, but she didn't hesitate to show up at our house to tell me she was fucking Kenny and was pregnant with his baby. One of them didn't like

Kenny and I was willing to bet that was Reggie. Because of this, I was starting to have hope in me and Kenny restoring our relationship. We'd both opened the door to the mess in our marriage but the two of them gave us a gentle push in the wrong direction.

Kenny stepped away from me and said, "Grandma is gonna be so excited to see y'all."

He glanced back at me, and I didn't see the hurt or hatred in his eyes. That gave me even more hope. He gave me a small smile, then said, "We'll talk more later."

"Okay."

I went outside and unloaded some of our clothes. The kids had clothes here, but I didn't have a stitch. I came back in the house and arranged some of their things then hopped in the shower. My desire to help Kenny get that fucker back was stronger than ever. Operation fuck that nigga up in full effect.

9

Kenny

I DIDN'T EXPECT HER TO LOOK THAT FUCKING GOOD. WHEN I got back home, Keisha was taking a pork roast from the oven. I'd taken it out the freezer last night to cook today. She looked up at me and said, "Hey."

"Hey."

She walked closer to me, giving me a view of the tight jeans she wore with the black, lace, low-cut camisole looking top and a see through, black and white striped shirt that she still had open. Her dreads were hanging loose, and her face was made up perfectly, her nose ring glittering. She had my dick getting hard. I hadn't bust a nut in a week, and I hadn't had sex in over a year. Kendrick took up all my free time. Plus, I was trying to rediscover myself without sex. After that period, I never did meet anyone else. I couldn't help but look her over. "Damn."

She blushed and said, "Thank you. I haven't cooked sides with the roast yet. I was getting the kids' things organized."

"You unloaded the entire trailer?"

"Yeah. I gotta bring it back."

"You always did extra shit. You know I always appreciated that, right?"

"I know, Kenny. You always told me how much you appreciated everything I did."

"Give me a chance to talk to the fellas about the truth of what happened, then you can move freely. My family ride deep for a nigga. I could see Storm approaching you about shit."

She rolled her eyes slightly, then chuckled. "I can see it, too."

"Keisha..."

I wanted to tell her that this changed everything. That I knew she didn't set out to stab me in the back, just like I didn't set out to betray her trust, either. We always understood one another. We'd both fucked up, but I wanted to try to rekindle what we once had. Before I could gather the nerve, my phone rang. That was probably a sign that I didn't need to make such a rushed decision like that. It was Storm calling. I guess we'd talked his ass up. "He's there?"

"Yeah. That muthafucka just walked in. I'm watching his ass flirt with the cashier on the monitor. I can't wait to get at his ass."

"A'ight. Keisha on her way."

She nodded at me, then grabbed her purse and keys and left out the door. "A'ight. I was worried about her staying there."

"Well, the plot thickens. Reggie set all this shit up. Everything from Shardae approaching me when I first cheated and hooking up with Keisha. She didn't take money from me to give to him. She'd taken it for her and the kids and somehow, he talked almost every dollar out of her hands."

"Well ain't that some shit. Wait 'til I tell Jasper and Ryder this shit. He always smiling at Tiff, too, so, Ryder ready to set shit off."

"Well, Keisha looking fine as fuck on her way up there. I almost said to hell with it and fucked the shit out of her. It's been a minute, so when I saw her a nigga was ready."

"I know we done got closer and shit, but nigga, I didn't wanna hear all that."

I chuckled as I shook my head. "Man, whatever. We gotta see you and Aspen all affectionate and shit. So, if we gotta be subjected to y'all shit, you can hear ours."

"Nigga, what the... Oh shit!"

"What?"

"What the fuck Keisha got on? Damn."

"A'ight, nigga! Watch your mouth."

He chuckled. I knew he was fucking with me. But Keisha looked damn good. "Has he seen her?"

"Looked at her when she walked through the door. I parked in back, so he don't know I'm here. He looking around now, like he tryna see if anybody here. He's walking over to her at the other cashier now."

"He took the bait. I'm gon' fuck him up tonight."

"We all gon' fuck his ass up."

"Yep. The kids are staying with Mama and Kendrick still with Tasha. Speaking of, I need to call to check on him. Let me know..."

"That muthafucka just rubbed his fingertips over her titty! I'm 'bout to go fuck him up now!"

"Storm, you gotta be fucking playing!"

"Not at all! He better be glad he's leaving. Bold muthafucka!"

"Tonight can't get here fast enough. What's Keisha doing?"

"She look like she's crying, bruh. I'm 'bout to go out there."

"Storm, be nice."

"I will, since I know the real. I mean... I'm never nice, but I'll be normal."

I rolled my eyes and ended the call. Reggie might die tonight. Once I went in on his ass, I may not be able to stop. Zayson had set that muthafucka up to where he had to get a tire repaired. He sat two glass bottles right by his tire at his house. That nigga rolled right over them. We knew he was gonna get the tire at Storm's shop. He'd always done business in Nome. He just didn't know what was up now and that we were on to his conniving ass. I was glad I wasn't up there. Although Keisha wasn't legally mine anymore, I would have fucked him up for what Storm said he'd done. If he was that bold with her, it was no wonder everybody knew about them to where it got back to Storm.

When I heard Keisha pull in the driveway, I opened the door and stood on the porch and watched her make her way to me. She looked at me and said, "He said to meet him at his house around eight. Is that cool?"

"Yeah. It'll be dark. Why were you crying?"

She lowered her head and said, "All I could think about was how much I regretted ever getting involved with him. I didn't know how I would react to seeing him again, but when I saw him, I felt disgusted that I'd stooped so low. He could never be you."

She gently stroked my cheek, then walked past me in the house. After closing the door, I caught up to her before she could hit the stairs and pulled her in my arms. "Will I have to be alone with him tonight?"

Pulling away from her, I said, "Naw. When he opens the door for you, his ass gon' get bumrushed by me, Storm, Ryder, and Jasper for sure. Zay fucked up his tire and Red kept watch, letting Storm know when he was coming to make sure he wasn't in the lobby. So, all you have to do is ring his doorbell and get him to open it. Once that happens, we in there."

"Okay. I'm kind of tired. If you don't mind, I'm gonna take a nap."

"That's fine. Don't forget you have to bring that trailer back."

"I won't."

I stepped away from her and watched her ascend the staircase. It was only two in the afternoon and U-Haul didn't close until seven. Going back to the couch, I sat and called Tasha. The phone rang a couple of times, then she answered, "Hello?"

"Hey. I was calling to check on Kendrick."

"He's good. He's a little cranky, but I think that's because he's tired. He hadn't had a nap yet."

"Okay. Well, I just wanted to check on him. I miss him already."

"You'll see him tomorrow night. Not much longer."

"Yeah. A'ight. I'll call and check on him later."

"For what?"

"That's what a good parent does."

"What are you saying, Kenny? That I'm not a good mother?"

"That's exactly what I'm saying, and the courts agreed with me. So, I'll check on him later."

"Whatever."

She ended the call. I was wondering when the real Tasha would show up. She was too nice last night and at the beginning of the call. I was ready for Kendrick to get to the age to where he could say whether he wanted to spend time with her or not. Taking a deep breath, I decided to go outside and ride my horse for a little while. I needed some peace.

❦

"Before you go in, I need you to stall a little, like drop your purse or something. That will assure that he won't have time to close the door before we get to his ass," Jasper said to Keisha as we got in our vehicles.

We were all in Storm's truck and would park down the road near Kortlynn's mother's house. Red had even hopped in with us. I think he just wanted to come to make sure we didn't go too far. Zay was at his mother-in-law's house and would meet up with us. Legend had gotten stuck with the kids, because Harper was at a wedding.

We all left U-Haul and followed Keisha to that fuck nigga's house. She seemed to be okay emotionally, although she seemed to be on the verge of crumbling earlier. When she turned on his street, we parked at the end of it and walked the rest of the way while she sat in her car, primping. Zay joined us and we all quickly made our way to his house, walking through people's yards. I didn't think this nigga had a clue what was about to happen. As I watched from the other side of the garage, Keisha got out of her car. And again, she stole my fucking breath, like I hadn't just seen her at U-Haul.

I could barely concentrate for shit. When she got close to me, wearing those black tights, high-heeled shoes, and a black and gold tank top, I couldn't help but grab her hand. "Shit, Keisha. For real?"

"He won't be able to turn this down, right? Kenny, I love you and whatever I gotta do for you, I'm gon' do that shit to the best of my abilities."

She put her hand to my face, and I pulled her to me by her waist as I stared in her eyes. Storm punched me in the arm. "Nigga get in headhunter frame of mind, so we can handle this nigga!" he whispered loudly.

I let Keisha go but we were still staring at one another for a moment. Before long, she was gon' get fucked and I was gon' enjoy every minute of having her again. Things were different and she and I would have a long talk about it tonight. She finally walked away, and Jasper said, "Reggie 'bout to know just how much weight the Henderson name carries. That weight finna be all on his ass!"

I peeked alongside the garage and Ryder was on the other side of the door, ready to give him the first one-two. Keisha went to ring the doorbell, then she hesitated. That had me cautious for a moment. Her shoulders lifted and fell, then she rang it. Ryder was right there waiting for that fool to open the door. As soon as he did, he smiled at Keisha and before she could stall or he could invite her in, Ryder snuck his ass. We all ran inside the house and Keisha closed the door while we beat the fuck out of his ass. "Y'all back up and let Kenny get a workout," Zay said.

When everybody backed up, I saw that Reggie had blood coming from his nose and mouth and he probably had a couple of broken ribs from the way he was holding his middle. I stared at his bitch-ass, and while I wanted to explain everything to him that I knew, I declined

78

to. If he was taking a beaten this bad, he had to have known that I knew everything. Not wasting anymore time, I kicked him in his mouth, then went to work on his ass while the fellas rooted me on. When I finally let up, he wasn't moving.

Keisha walked over to him and checked his pulse. "It's still strong as hell. I can't believe I let you fucking convince me to betray my husband. Not only that, but his money... I was so stupid!" she screamed.

Everyone was quiet as hell, watching her nearly have a breakdown. She stood to her feet and spit on him as she looked at him in disgust, knowing that everything they shared was a game. Zay and Jasper picked him up from the floor and brought him to his room, throwing his ass in there. When they came out, we all left. I couldn't take a chance of walking Keisha to her car, so I went with the fellas, the same way I'd gotten there.

As we drove back to Nome, I couldn't stop my mind from racing. Between what we did tonight and whether Keisha was trustworthy or not. I didn't understand how she could go from treating me like shit to being all distraught and remorseful within a matter of minutes. It made it seem like she was only behaving that way because of what I knew. "Nigga, you quiet. You regretting what we did?" Jasper asked.

"Naw. I'm just tryna figure Keisha out. I don't wanna take her back only to find out she a shady muthafucka. I done been fucked over enough, and I'm scared that I might kill her ass if I find out anything else she's done."

"Have a talk with her. Ask her if there's anything else you need to know. Make her ass come clean about everything and you do the same. That's the only way that shit gon' work. You obviously love her. Shit, nigga, you my fucking role model," Red said.

Jasper, Storm, and Ryder laughed and agreed. "Well, in case y'all forgot, I ain't innocent, either. I got a one-year-old son to prove it. I love Keisha with everything in me. She's the only woman I've ever loved, real shit. Call me soft, sprung, or whatever the fuck y'all wanna call me, but I played a significant role in where we are right now. What she did with Reggie was in response to that shit with Shardae."

"I can't believe you slept with that bitch. You know she couldn't hardly stand us in school," Jasper said.

"She was just a hater, because she knew we were the shit and wasn't checking for her ass. That's all. Plus, we were kids then. We all grown as hell, now," I replied.

"Here is what the fuck I wanna know," Storm said.

"Aww, shit. Here come the fuckery," Ryder said while shaking his head.

Everybody chuckled because we all knew Storm just said whatever the fuck came to his mind. He was serious, though, never cracked a smile. "You fucked all them bitches raw?"

Everybody's eyebrows shot up, but they were all looking at me, waiting on an answer. I gave them a one-cheeked smile. "I wore condoms with Shardae, but one of them bitches broke. I mean, I *am* a Henderson, right?"

"Hell to the fucking yeah," Jasper added as everybody laughed.

"With Brandy..." I felt the worst about her. She was the one that had an abortion. My guilt about her ate me alive. "She was a virgin."

"Nigga, what?" Ryder said.

"I met her at the post office in China. She was so beautiful. So, I discreetly handed her a business card for the rice farms, that I'd circled my number on. You know they have Daddy's number on there, too. She called me within an hour. She was only twenty-three. But when she told me she was a virgin, I almost left her alone. I feel like shit for seducing her and that happened almost four years ago. She fell in love with me, and I don't even know how. I never took her anywhere and I didn't spend a lot of time with her because *I* didn't wanna catch feelings. She eventually stopped having sex with me, especially when she did her research and found out I was married."

"Damn, Kenny. How you know she aborted the baby?" Red asked.

"She called me about two months after we started fucking and

IN WAY TOO DEEP

said she was pregnant, but she refused to have my baby. Honestly, I didn't want her to have my baby, either. It would be a constant reminder of the fuck shit I did to her. I dipped in raw because she was a virgin. I had to feel that shit. Nobody I'd slept with had been a virgin, so the fuckboy came out in me. I brought her to the abortion clinic and paid for everything. Keisha saw us together at the clinic."

I shook my head slowly at the recollection. "After that day, I never heard from her again."

"Damn," Ryder said.

"Nigga don't stop now. Tasha hoe ass. You had to know she was a hoe, 'cause I knew she threw the pussy at you."

"She caught me off guard at the convenience store that day Jasper walked in on us. She got pregnant from pre-nut. Had to, because when Jasper walked in on us, I didn't finish. That was the only time I fucked her raw."

"I know that's Kendrick mama, and I love that lil boy, but that bitch was after anybody with money. She tried to holla at me, Jasper, and Legend."

"She was on her way to me, too, until Shana cut her off. Y'all know Shana don't play that shit. She would have fucked her up while she was pregnant," Red added.

We all laughed as we went through the light in Nome. Storm hopped the railroad tracks to drop Red off. The minute he got out, Storm said, "Y'all know that snitch nigga might report us. Y'all ready to deal with that heat?"

"We all own our own shit. That shit ain't gon' stop our money. Well... except Ryder. But bruh, you know we got'chu, right?" Jasper asked.

"Of course. But I can't stand that muthafucka, either. He been tryna get at Tiffany. She don't think I know, though. I caught him before her first barebacking event and before we went to Vegas at the washateria. So, whatever comes with the couple of kicks I got in, I'm ready for it."

I slapped his hand, then asked Storm, "Is there a reason why you passed up our houses to drop off Red first?"

"Y'all my brothers. Don't get me wrong, Red like a brother, too, but I wanted to talk to y'all about some shit. Ryder, you married in the family, so you family and this shit might affect Tiff, so we need to do something."

We all frowned, trying to figure out what the fuck he was talking about. "Marcus might be up to some bullshit again."

I rolled my eyes and took a deep breath. "You don't want WJ in on this conversation?"

"Fuck WJ. I got some shit on his ass, too. So, whenever y'all free to talk, we need to. Kenny, I know you got some shit to handle with Keisha, but we all need to talk sooner rather than later."

I shook my head slowly. I didn't know what the fuck was going on, but Storm always had his fucking ear to the street. Hopefully, whatever he knew didn't have us turning against our own blood.

K 10 K

K eisha

AS I SAT IN THE DRIVEWAY WAITING ON KENNY, I COULDN'T believe what I'd witnessed tonight. Kenny had never been one to fight... that I knew of anyway. I could clearly tell that it wasn't his first time, though. Being in his arms felt amazing and I couldn't believe how I'd fucked that up. When I saw the headlights behind me, I got out my car and fixed my clothes. Kenny had been showing me some things today that insinuated he might be ready to work things out. I was happy but nervous at the same time.

When he got out of Storm's truck, I stared at him, not being able to look away. He went straight to the door, only glancing at me. That put me on edge. Going to the door as he unlocked it, I realized he'd made a phone call. "It's eight-thirty. He should be asleep," he said calmly.

He must have been talking to Tasha. What caught me off-guard was when I heard him say, "I should have known better than messing with a ratchet bitch like you. Kendrick is our only topic of discussion, so stay the fuck out of my business."

My sweet, soft-spoken Kenny was long gone. I missed that side of him, but I knew he was tired of being ran over and had finally come out of his shell. He was reminding me so much of Jasper and Storm right now. I sat quietly on the couch and listened to him curse Tasha from here to fucking Australia, before he ended the call. When he did, he stood there and took a couple of deep breaths. He turned to look at me, then walked over and sat. He grabbed my hand and the warmth from his touch surged throughout my body.

While I missed his soft, tender side, this roughneck shit he was on was turning me on as well. "Keisha, I need to know something. But before I ask the question, I need to feel your lips. Can I?"

"You can have whatever you want, Kenny."

He leaned in and gently placed his lips on mine. His hand went to the back of my neck, pulling me in deeper as he slid his tongue in my mouth. It felt like I was about to cum just from his touch. I hadn't experienced this from him in over two years, and God, it was amazing. He pulled away and my eyes remained closed. "Keisha, how was it so easy to flip the script and start being nice to me?"

"Because it was an act. I'd gotten used to being hateful towards you. As long as you didn't know about what I'd done, I couldn't be all friendly with you like it didn't matter that our marriage of twelve years had gone down the drain. Now that I know you know, I can drop the act."

I lowered my head in embarrassment, but Kenny lifted it by my chin. "I still love you, Keisha. As much as I wanted to hate you, I can't. And believe me, I've tried."

He smiled at me and it melted my insides. I quickly hugged his neck. "I love you, too, Kenny. While I've had time to rebuild my trust in you, I know you haven't had time to do the same for what I've done. I'm going to try to give you that time."

84

"Let's not jump the gun. I'm not pursuing a relationship yet. Like you said, I still don't quite trust you. I need to know... is there anything else that you've withheld from me that you think I need to know?"

My eyes pleaded with him, because there was one other thing. I never wanted to tell him, and I'd refused to all these years. It was too late to say that there was nothing, because he'd seen my reaction to his words. "What is it?"

He scooted away from me and I avoided his gaze. "Umm... WJ..."

"What about WJ?!" he boomed.

His outburst scared the shit out of me. I nearly hopped off the sofa. "He umm... he came on to me a couple of times. Once, early in our marriage before Karima and again after."

Kenny stood from the couch and calmly walked toward the staircase. But when he went in that closet, before he even got to what he went in there to get, my eyebrows rose. He turned around with a shotgun in his hand and pumped that shit and began loading it with shells from the shelf. "Kenny? What are you doing?"

"I'm going fuck that muthafucka up."

"No! That's why I never wanted to tell you. That's your brother!"

I quickly grabbed my phone and called Jasper. He only lived a couple of houses down. "Hello?"

"Jasper, hurry and get here. Now!"

I dropped the phone and stepped in front of Kenny. "Get the fuck out the way!" he yelled at me.

"Kenny! Please!"

He pushed past me, almost knocking me to the floor. When he opened the door, I saw headlights. *Thank God.* That had to be Jasper. He only lived a couple of houses down. I ran after Kenny and saw Jasper and Storm both approaching. "Bruh, what the fuck going on?" Storm asked.

"Yo' bitch-ass brother 'bout to catch a hot one in his mutha-fucking ass."

"Naw. That shit ain't finna go down. We gon' talk like adults. That's our brother," Jasper said as another car drove in the driveway.

It was Ryder. He and Tiffany lived a few houses down as well. When he walked up, Kenny cursed. "Fuck!"

He turned and went back in the house, blowing by me like I wasn't there. He flopped down on the couch and I sat next to him. "Naw. Get the fuck away from me."

I felt like I stopped breathing. "Kenny…"

"Naw. You should have kept that shit to yo'self. 'Cause I wanna kill my brother. That shit is eating me alive. I'd rather you lie to me than tell me some shit like that. Get the fuck away from me!"

The tears dropped from my eyes uncontrollably as I got up and ran up the stairs while the fellas stared in disbelief. I ran to the room I slept in last night and fell on the bed. How was I supposed to lie to him? What would I have said? He would have known that I was lying. As I cried, holding my face in my hands so I didn't get makeup on the comforter, there was a knock on the doorframe. I looked up to see Jasper standing there. "Come back downstairs, Keisha. We need to get to the bottom of this shit."

I nodded, then stood from the bed. When I got to him, he rested his hand on my back. Had that been Storm, I would've been scared he was gonna push me down the stairs. When we reached where the guys were, they all looked at me with frowns on their faces. "Why in the fuck would you say something now? You should have told him when it first happened."

I snapped on Storm's ass. "Y'all don't understand the fucking position I'm in! What the fuck? Kendrall," I started by staring at him, "… asked me if there was anything else I needed to tell him. My eyes give away every damn thing when I'm not prepared. He saw in my eyes that there was something else that I was keeping from him. Had I lied and he found out about it, where would that have left me? Huh? I was trying to keep the peace between him and y'all, his brothers, especially because he always felt like he didn't belong."

I snatched my purse off the countertop and walked out the

fucking door. They reminded me of all those people that criticized women for finally talking about a rape that happened years before. Getting in my car, I realized I couldn't go any damn where because I was blocked in. But tonight, I guess I would be sleeping in my car. I leaned the seat back and got comfortable. Kenny was too angry to invite me back in the house anyway. Tomorrow, I would go to Beaumont and try to find a job and somewhere to live. I had enough money to pay about three months of rent somewhere, but in the meantime, I would get a hotel room.

I knew Kenny needed time and me staying there was only gonna make things more difficult. Turning my back to the house, I went to sleep.

❦

THAT KNOCKING NOISE WAS GETTING ON MY DAMN NERVES. I saw when Ryder, Storm and Jasper left, but I was too sleepy to leave the house tonight. I would have fallen asleep at the wheel on my way to Beaumont. Now Kenny was knocking on the glass. It had to be midnight. He didn't come out right after they left, so I'd fallen asleep. "Keisha, come in the house."

I squeezed my eyes shut, not wanting to go back inside to let him verbally assault me any longer. When the doors unlocked and he opened the door, I was shocked. I should have known he had a key to my vehicle, though. "Come in the house," he said softly.

"I'm fine sleeping here. Tomorrow, I will be out of your hair."

"What do you mean?"

"I'm getting a room in Beaumont."

"Naw. You staying here. Now get in the house before I carry you in there."

"You are confusing as hell, Kenny. Please just leave me here until you know what you want."

Before I could say anything else, he yanked my ass out the car and threw me over his shoulder like I was a dead deer. The tears left my eyes because I was emotional as hell. I didn't know what to think about all the shit that had gone down tonight. When we got inside, Kenny let me down, then locked the door. I quickly made my way upstairs and went to the bathroom to clean the makeup from my face and change into some bed clothes.

WJ was a world class fuck up. I wondered if he'd flirted with Aspen or Chasity. The first time he did it when I'd met Kenny at the grass farm, he'd mumbled that I was fine as shit. I had to ask him to repeat himself because I knew I had to have imagined that shit. But that bold-ass nigga repeated himself. I was so shocked, I was literally silent the rest of the evening. The second time he did it, Karima was probably a year old. He'd said that someone as fine as me was worth a married man cheating on his wife. It took everything in me not to pop the shit out of him.

Not only was he disrespecting his wife, but he was disrespecting his brother as well. After that instance, he didn't mess with me anymore, because I told him if he said anything else, I would tell Kenny. I didn't understand how he would be cool with flirting with his own sister-in-law or how he thought I would be cool with that shit, either. As I slid on my silk pajama pants, there was a knock at the door. Taking a deep breath, I opened it to find Kenny standing there. "I'm sorry for my behavior tonight. It just caught me off-guard. It makes sense, though. He was there when I talked to everyone about helping me with Reggie. He didn't want to be apart and he's refused to talk to me since you've been back, like he knows that its gonna come out, since everything else has."

I nodded and walked past him to the bedroom. I was tired as hell. Before I could enter the room, though, Kenny grabbed my hand and pulled me toward his bedroom. "Kenny..."

"I'm not tryna have sex, Keisha. I just miss having you in bed with me... holding you. That's all I want... well... that's all I'm trying to pursue tonight."

I stared at him for a moment, then decided against it. "It's not a good idea, Kenny. I'll talk to you tomorrow."

He allowed my hand to slide from his, then nodded and went to his room. Sleeping in the bed with him without doing anything else would be too hard for me. His dick was hard when he kissed me, so I knew it would be hard if I laid in that bed with him, allowing him to hold me in his arms. It took everything in me not to reach out and touch it. Closing the door, I got in bed and laid there, thinking about what I would do tomorrow. If I got a hotel room, I wouldn't wanna leave the kids. I already missed them. They rarely stayed away from home, but I was sure they were having the time of their lives with their grandparents and cousins.

Grabbing my phone from the nightstand, I decided to text Cass. I hadn't talked to her since last night when Kenny had gone off on me and snatched the phone. It was after midnight, but since it was a Saturday, I knew she was awake. *Kenny kissed me.*

I rolled over to my back and stared at the ceiling. Had he left me in the car, I would have been knocked out. Since I'd washed my face and moved around, I couldn't sleep now. My phone chimed, so I lifted it from my chest to see, *Bitch, you lying!*

I chuckled, because I could hear Cass saying that in my head and I could imagine her facial expression. *Nope. It was passionate. I wanted him to fuck me so bad. He wants me back. I know he does.*

Well, bitch, duh! That nigga didn't fall out of love with you because you pissed him off. Call me!

I shook my head and placed the call, telling myself not to get too excited where Kenny would be able to hear me. "Bitch, how did that shit happen?"

"We were sitting on the couch after we got back to the house from... you know." I couldn't afford to say it aloud, not knowing if Kenny was eavesdropping like last time. "I suppose the events of the night and what I wore had him sensitive to me. He kissed me. I hadn't felt a kiss like that from him in almost two years."

"Damn. Well, why did y'all stop?"

"We started talking about WJ's trifling ass."

I explained to Cass what had happened and how I ended up

89

telling him about WJ and then what happened afterwards. I was still somewhat upset about it. I was always told not to ask a question if you don't know if you'll be able to handle the answer. By the time I ran down everything to Cass, she said, "Ain't that some bullshit. For once, I'm actually on your side about this one."

I shook my head. "Well, it's about fucking time. He apologized and wanted me to sleep in the bed with him tonight."

"Where are the kids?"

"Their grandparents' house."

"So, what's the problem?"

"He doesn't want sex right now. He just wants to hold me. You know as well as I do, if I feel Kenny's hard dick against my ass, I'm gonna hop his bones."

"Without question wit' yo' horny ass."

"Shut up, Cass."

"Just take it slow. Follow his lead, Keisha. I know you want your man back but give him time."

"Yeah. He and I were targeted. Reggie and Kenny were friends at one time. He set us both up and we fell for it, Cass. That hurts. I wanted to kill his ass. Where would me and Kenny be right now if we hadn't have fallen for that bullshit?"

The tears escaped me without warning and I couldn't hide my cries. We were both fools. "Girl, if you don't stop all that crying. That shit made the both of you stronger. Yeah, it's gon' be a battle, but you're both built to handle it. Just put in the work, Keisha."

There was a knock at the door, so I said, "I'll call you tomorrow, okay? Kenny's at the door."

"Okay. I love you, girl, and I miss you already."

"I love and miss you, too."

I ended the call and went to the door, opening it to find Kenny standing there. He walked in the room and closed the door behind him, then came straight to me, pulling me to his chest and hugging me tightly. I wrapped my arms around his waist and cried into his chest. Tipping my head back, he kissed my lips, then led me to the bed. "Come on, baby. Let's get some rest."

I laid in bed and he followed me, pulling me in his arms. Lying on his chest, I continued crying my eyes out. It wasn't a cry of sadness, though. I was happy to be back in his arms and that everything was finally out in the open. I just hoped he was able to forget about this whole thing with WJ.

11

K enny

"So, you telling me that muthafucka is tryna overturn Daddy's businesses with Marcus?" Jasper asked Storm.

"Naw. But he gave Marcus information to do that shit on his own. Betraying ass muthafucka. Running his fucking mouth for no damn reason. WJ can't be no fucking Henderson. He like Scar from the fucking Lion King. Wanna run shit but ain't even a percentage of what Mufasa is."

"I'm mad that you comparing this shit to the Lion King," Ryder said.

I chuckled. Storm was a big kid at heart, but only the family got to see that. Ryder was just getting a glimpse. "Thank y'all for coming through last night. I wanted to go fuck him up. I still do."

"How are you and Keisha?" Ryder asked.

"Good. I held her in my arms all night last night."

"Aww shit. Y'all fucked already?" Storm asked.

"No, nigga. I said I held her in my arms all night. I ain't say shit about fucking."

Jasper chuckled. "So, what we gon' do? We have to get Pops involved."

"We do. As far as Kenny's situation, I think he needs to approach that nigga about it. We can be yo' backup Kenny. You know how WJ ass is. Always ready to fight."

"Sound like all y'all asses. Always ready to fight or shoot. Tiffany just like y'all. I keep having to remind lil baby that she pregnant. She wanted to come meet with us today," Ryder said while shaking his head. "If she knew all this shit, she was gon' wanna fuck WJ up herself."

We all laughed. Tiff was no joke and she was the closest to the three of us out of our sisters. Jenahra and Chrissy pretty much did their own thing. "So, when are we going talk to Dad?" I asked.

"When we leave here. Marcus needs to quit tripping. Since the shit hit the fan, Pops dropped the charges against him and we allowed him to learn the business, accepting him as a Henderson, but he got the nerve to still be on some bullshit," Jasper said.

"Hell yeah. Had that muthafucka working at my shop and everything. He ain't getting no fucking sympathy. Can't give a nigga shit. They always want more."

"Well, I ain't gon' be with y'all to talk to Pops, 'cause I gotta get to the shop. Make sure Tiffany don't try to come in y'all meeting. Y'all fill me in later."

"A'ight, bruh," we all said at different moments.

I couldn't believe Marcus was tryna fuck up shit. None of us really talked to him that much, but we weren't rude, either. After all the bullshit a few years ago, I didn't trust him. He hung around WJ the most and now I knew why. "Storm, how you always find shit out?" I asked.

"Cuz niggas scared of what's gon' happen if I find out on my own. So, they run their mouths and tell me all the shit I need to know."

I rolled my eyes. "Whatever. Give me a minute to go back home and check on Keisha and call Tasha. She supposed to be bringing Kendrick back today. I don't need no confusion with her ass."

"I'm still pissed about Tasha. Anybody but her ass. Why her ass?" Jasper asked.

"You really have to ask?"

"I guess not. Meet us back here in an hour."

"A'ight."

I left Jasper's barbershop and headed back home. When I got there and walked through the door, Keisha was coming down the stairs with a duffle bag. "Where you going?"

"I'm gonna get a room, Kenny. I can't have another night like last night. I want you so bad, but I don't wanna rush you."

"Man, if you don't go put that shit back in the room. I'ma grown ass man. If I don't want you, I know how to stop you. But you staying here. Understood?"

Truth was I still had some trust issues with her. I didn't know if she was telling me everything or if she was sincere about what she *was* telling me. So, I needed to keep her ass close to me. "Yeah," she said and headed back upstairs.

It took a lot of restraint to not fuck her last night, but as long as I was doubting her, I'd keep my dick to myself. I'd been doing that shit for a while now anyway. Going to the kitchen, I opened the pack of ground beef and began browning it. I thought we could have nachos tonight. Eating a big meal wasn't on my agenda of things to do. I was hoping everybody else was feeling me. The kids would probably be fine with it, though. When Keisha came back downstairs, I pulled her to me roughly and held her face to mine by her chin. "You belong here. If anything changes, I'll let you know."

"You mean if you still don't trust me after a certain amount of time?"

"Since you want me to be blunt, that's exactly right. If I find out something you aren't telling me or if you're lying to me, you'll be out of here on the first thing smoking... alone. I want to believe you telling me the truth and that you're sincere with how you're feeling. I really do, but my mind keeps telling me to wait. It wants me to be cautious when dealing with you. My heart has to sit this one out."

She looked hurt, but she asked the question. After staring at me for a couple of seconds, she turned on her heels and went back upstairs. I didn't know what she wanted me to do. This shit was hard for me. Extremely hard. I was almost willing to bet that when I left to go meet my brothers, she would be gone. This feeling was foreign to me. Although Keisha had cheated on me, I'd never felt like I couldn't trust her. Even with the revelations of how Reggie had orchestrated this whole shit, those feelings were still there, and they only got stronger when she accused WJ of flirting with her. I just didn't know what to do about how I was feeling.

After I'd finished the ground beef, I went upstairs to find her lying in the bed, playing on her phone. She sat up when I walked in. Sitting on the bed beside her, I said, "I don't know where to start. I've always trusted you, but with these new revelations, especially about WJ, it's hard. I'm gonna confront him today. I wanna put all this shit behind me. I really do. We can go to counseling to see if that helps. I still love you with everything in me, Keisha. You're still the only woman I *want* to love. Please, just give me time. You leaving isn't gonna help me, though."

I slid my finger down her face and I could see the hurt in her eyes. After kissing her forehead, I said, "I'm about to leave to go meet up with Storm and Jasper so we can talk to Pops and WJ. Please be here when I get back. I'll have the kids with me, too."

"What are you doing with the ground beef?"

"Nachos. That cool?"

"Yeah."

As I turned to go back downstairs, Keisha said, "Kenny."

"Yeah?"

I turned back to her and she slid her hands up my chest to my face and pulled it to hers. She kissed me slowly, making me wanna forget about everything I'd just said. For her to still cause a stirring in

MONICA WALTERS

me that deeply, I knew we couldn't let go. We were in way too deep. She pulled away from me, but I pulled her back as my hands slid down to her ass. When I separated my lips from hers, I said, "I'm trying."

"I know. I'll be more patient. I'm trying, too. I love you."

"I love you, too. I'll bring some chips back."

"Okay."

For some reason, I was still standing there. It was like every amazing moment we had found a way to flash through my mind like a movie. From the day in the grocery store parking lot, to her moving to Nome, pregnant with KJ and us getting married. We had amazing times. When they were building the convenience store, she and I spent a lot of time together, making sure things were running smoothly. Our lives were so perfect. I knew with time we would be okay. However, one thing would have to change. We would have to talk to one another and stop bottling shit up that could potentially destroy everything we built together.

I finally got the nerve to leave, but Keisha held me tightly around my waist as she rested her forehead against my shoulder. I kissed her head and said, "Don't worry. I believe that everything will work out for the best. As long as we talk to each other. That was our biggest downfall."

"It was. This time around, we will be so much stronger and better for each other."

When she let me go, I slipped away from her and went to meet my brothers.

❧

"So y'all are telling me that Marcus is trying to fuck up what I worked hard for and WJ is helping his ass?"

I knew Pops was mad as hell, because he never used harsh language like that. The word was that he was a lot like Storm when he was a young man and that's where Storm got his temper from. It

96

was hard to believe until now. He was pacing back and forth, running his hand down his curly black hair. "Word is that Marcus is planning to plant a different grass in the hayfields when they disc them in a couple of months. WJ has been telling him all our practices and everything. So, he's been putting his plan together. He even talking 'bout tryna fuck with the cattle again."

"Seven, how do you know all this?"

"This guy that I'm cool with, been watching his ass for me. I ain't never trusted his ass. He was doing good at first, but now, that muthafucka back up to his shenanigans. He wants to take over this shit, but I don't know how he think he gon' beat all of us out of what we worked hard for, too. He gon' catch a bullet in his fucking throat."

"Let's go talk to WJ. We have to get to the bottom of this shit, today. Why is he telling Marcus all the inner workings of the business when Marcus hasn't really expressed an interest in much of anything?" Dad asked.

"Same thing I was wondering," I said.

We all hopped in Storm's truck and went to WJ's tractor business. I had a feeling this shit was about to get ugly. Dad had told us to let him do all the talking, but I could see in Storm's eyes that he was ready to fire off. When we walked around back, WJ was underneath a tractor and oil was every damn where. We all stood there patiently as my phone vibrated in my pocket. After checking it, I saw a message from Tasha, saying she was on her way with Kendrick. That gave me forty minutes to get home to meet her. Once WJ slid from under the tractor, he looked at us with wide eyes. "Y'all scared the hell out of me."

"WJ, you know I ain't ever been one to beat around the bush, especially with none of y'all. What are you and Marcus up to?" Dad asked.

WJ frowned hard, then asked, "What'chu mean?"

"Why are you feeding Marcus information about the hay fields and the inner workings of the business?"

"He told me he wanted to be apart when we started planting. So, I was telling him how we did things."

"Why did he need to know who our most demanding customers were? That shit ain't none of his business," Storm said.

Dad cut his eyes at Storm, stopping him dead in his tracks. We all looked back at WJ. His face was red, and I knew he was about to lie. That nigga always turned red when he was about to lie. "Look. Marcus was left out of a lot of shit. He deserves to have a piece of the pie as much as we do."

Before I could interfere, Storm had punched that nigga dead in his mouth. I held Storm back and Jasper held WJ. Dad stood in the middle and he said to WJ, "You done really fucked up. We will talk in private with your mama."

Storm jerked away from me, but I had to get my piece out. "I have an issue with you, too. Keisha said you flirted with her on more than one occasion. Tell me you ain't a backstabbing muthafucka."

"What? That bitch is lying. She ain't even that fine."

Evidently, Storm didn't hit his ass hard enough, so I came back with a two-piece for him. "You a fucking liar. Stay away from my family. You step foot on my property and I'm gon' shoot yo' big ass."

I jerked away from Storm, who was now holding me, and walked off to the truck. My own brother had disrespected my woman. His voice had elevated in pitch and everything. If he could double cross Dad, then I knew that none of us were off-limits. I slowly shook my head in disbelief, because that nigga didn't value his life. When Pops, Storm, and Jasper joined me, they were all quiet. I think we were all in disbelief. I would have never accused WJ of being a backstabbing, evil muthafucka, but yet, here we were. I owed Keisha an apology. I owed her my trust. "Kenny, you alright?" my dad asked.

"Naw. My big brother is a snake. One of the people I've looked up to my entire life is a low-down muthafucka. How could he flirt with my wife? She was my wife and he was tryna hit? That's some bullshit. Although he denied it, I could tell he was lying."

"We all could tell he was lying," Jasper added. "And we all looked up to him. None of us thought he was perfect, but I would have never thought he was capable of turning against us like we don't mean shit to him. It makes me wonder what else he may have done."

"I bet that nigga was involved with Marcus when all that shit went down about the cattle. You never knew when I was gon' pop up out there. Somebody had to be telling Marcus when to go out there. That bitch ain't my brother no more," Storm said.

For the first time ever, I saw my dad drop a tear. He was hurt that WJ could turn on us. I needed a damn drink. Storm pat his shoulder and said, "We got'chu, Daddy. I know this shit hurts, but we here for you. Okay?"

"I know, Seven. I just don't know what I did wrong to where WJ is turning against me... against us. Why? I don't understand it."

"None of us do. But all we can do is react accordingly," Jasper said.

When Storm dropped me off at the store, Shylou was coming out. He had some papers in his hand with a smile on his face. "What's up, bruh?"

"You got the loan! I called Price and told him the news, too. He's waiting to hear from you on when you wanna break ground. I'm proud of you, Kenny. The biggest truck stop from Beaumont to Houston gon' be in country ass Nome, Texas!"

"But you gon' get off big city Nome, though! Thanks, bruh. You sure you don't wanna remain a partner? You can always be a silent partner."

"Let me think on that."

I hugged him as I took the papers from him and walked in the store to go to my office for a moment. The shit with WJ had kind of put a damper on my excitement, but to hell with those nachos. I was taking my family out to celebrate when Kendrick got here. I could sign papers tomorrow at the bank. Going back to my truck, I hopped in to pick up KJ and Karima, then head home, so I could be there when Tasha got there.

12

K eisha

"Maybe she got held up," I said as Kenny paced.

Kendrick was supposed to be here over two hours ago, and Tasha wasn't answering her phone. I was trying to remain positive and keep Kenny in a good head space. He was so happy when he first got here about being approved to expand his convenience store into something amazing. He'd kissed me on the lips in front of the kids. But now he was angry and worried, and that was causing me to be angry as well. I never thought I would be able to handle raising someone else's child with Kenny, but if I wanted him back, I would have to accept it.

"She being conniving and trifling."

Just as he said that, the doorbell rang. The kids were already eating nachos though, because they'd gotten hungry. Our dinner plans were ruined, and Kenny was pissed. He flung the door open and she cowered in his presence. He picked up Kendrick as he said, "Da-da!"

Kenny kissed his head, then put him down. He ran straight to the table with the kids, but I noticed he was dirty. Staying in place, I knew I needed to watch Kenny to be sure he didn't strangle the fuck out of Tasha. I'd gladly do that shit for him, though. "Where the fuck you been?" he asked in a low and deadly voice.

Okay, maybe the kids needed to get out of here. "KJ and Karima, y'all go upstairs and take Kendrick with you. KJ, can you start him some bath water running?"

"Yes, ma'am."

He'd been so mild-mannered since we'd been back. I was thankful for that. Once they were upstairs, I walked closer to Kenny and Tasha to hear her say, "He's my fucking son, too. I should be able to keep him as long as I want!"

"That's your fault why you can't. I would have been fine with the time change if you would've called and said something, though. I was sitting here worried that something had happened to him."

"What about me? You weren't worried about something happening to me?"

"I don't give a fuck about you, Tasha."

"Oh, but you gave a good fuck when you was diving in my pussy."

Before Kenny could grab her, I stepped in front of him. "Kendrick is home. Just let it go. He needs y'all to be able to get along. Although, he's young, he can sense your attitudes towards one another. Please."

Tasha rolled her eyes and dropped his duffle bag and walked off. Kenny wrapped his arms around me and kissed the side of my head. "Thank you, Keisha, 'cause I was finna snatch her ass up. I hate that I fucked her. What in the fuck was I thinking? Why didn't I force you to talk to me? Fuck!"

I turned around in his arms and gently rubbed his face. "We can't dwell in the past, baby. Let's just move forward. I wanna move forward with you, the first and only man to steal my heart. I love you, Kenny."

He pulled my face to his, then said, "I didn't wanna say this in front of the kids, but I apologize for not really believing you at first. WJ is a whole bitch for the shit he did. So, I hope we can go to counseling and get this thing together. I know dealing with Tasha is gonna be hard for you and I'll do my best to shield you from her dramatics. I love you, too."

I hugged him tightly, then pulled away from him. "I'm gonna go check on the kids."

"I'm right behind you. I need to bathe Kendrick."

"I can wash him, Kenny."

That last statement rendered us both speechless for a moment. Once we reached the landing of the staircase, I said, "Maybe we can go out tomorrow after the kids get out of school. I'm sure they're excited about reuniting with their friends."

He pulled me in his arms again. "You're amazing. I know being around Kendrick is hard for you."

"Not that hard since he looks like you and our kids. Had he looked like her, it would be harder. It's not his fault, though. He's innocent."

He nodded, then said, "Tomorrow, I promised to take KJ to the herd to cut. He wants to enter the rodeo circuit doing that."

"Refresh my memory. What exactly is it?"

"Umm... it's pretty much keeping one cow isolated from the herd. It almost looks like he and the horse are playing defense in a football or soccer game against the cow. Look at this video."

He pulled up his YouTube app and showed me a video of someone cutting. I nodded as I watched. I remembered seeing him and KJ do that when they were doctoring the cattle. I didn't know it was a whole rodeo event. "Oh okay. Well, we all may come out and watch."

"Okay. Maybe we can go out on the weekend. I have to sign the paperwork and get with Price about doing the dirt work."

"Okay."

I headed to the bathroom to find KJ had put Kendrick in the tub and was entertaining him. Looking at the floor, I noticed his diaper was sopping wet and had shit in it like he hadn't been changed all day. I slowly shook my head as KJ noticed that I'd entered the bathroom. "Mama, he's filthy."

"Thanks, Kendrall. I'll take it from here."

"Okay."

Unlike Kenny, KJ didn't mind being called Kendrall. He actually liked that name. When I walked to Kendrick, he smiled at me and handed me his plastic basketball. I smiled back and began washing him up. This poor child. His skin was sticky, and his hair hadn't been brushed since he left. He even had spaghetti sauce in it. Well, at least the bitch fed him. After washing his hair, I got him out of the tub and dried him off, then moisturized his little body. When I put on his diaper and pajamas, he kissed my cheek. I couldn't help but hug him and show him the love he was so easily showing me. After kissing his cheek, I turned to see Kenny watching us. His face was red from his emotions.

Kendrick ran to him and he picked him up. "You smell good, man."

"Da-Da, I shweep."

He laid his head on Kenny's shoulder as I smiled softly. "Thank you, Keisha."

I nodded, then started the shower. Before he walked out, he said, "You can shower in our room, baby."

I smiled at him and turned the shower off as he walked away. We were going to make this work. I could feel it in my bones. Regardless of our past, we were ready to be a family again.

"Honestly, I'm glad you're back. I know you and Kenny have a lot of shit to work through, especially with Tasha's triflin' ass, but I feel like this is where you belong," Tiffany said.

She clearly didn't know all the details and I wasn't going to be the one to tell her. I'd come to Mom and Dad Henderson's house to say hello and to thank them for the seafood they sent our way. Kenny and KJ had been spending a lot of time practicing and he and I were getting used to one another again. We hadn't had sex yet and I was content with exhibiting patience. We'd already had our second appointment with a counselor last week, and I was beyond happy to be moving in a positive direction with him.

Tiffany had showed up just as I was leaving. She stopped to fuss at me for not making time to see her. She'd only been working at the washateria lately. I had to get to the schools to get the kids and Kenny had Kendrick with him, so he wouldn't be irritable waiting in line at Karima's school. They'd been back at their schools for the past month and they were loving it. As I drove in line, I immediately got scared. I saw Reggie standing under the awning with his arm in a sling. Grabbing my phone, I called Kenny. "Hey, baby. What's up?"

"Reggie is at the school."

"Don't panic, baby. If he wanted to press charges, he would have by now. Hopefully, he's not crazy enough to say anything to you. Not unless he has a death wish."

"I hope you're right."

"Don't worry. I have a nice lil setup for you when you get home. I'm taking the kids with me when y'all get home. We'll do homework and get something to eat, then bring you something back."

"What kind of setup?" I asked, feeling excited.

"You'll see when you get here."

I ended the call in the best mood ever, forgetting all about Reggie until the line started moving. He was still standing there and when I got close, he saw me. His face turned serious and he refused to look at me again. When I got to the front, practically parked right where he was standing, he opened the car door. My nerves were on edge until I saw Karima coming out of the school. She quickly made her way to the car and said, "Thanks Officer Reggie!"

"You're welcome! Have a good day!"

He closed the door and I immediately took off without waiting for Karima to buckle up. "Mommy, Officer Reggie says he knows my whole family. He named you and Daddy, Aunt Tiffany, Uncle Jasper, Uncle Storm..."

She was going on and on, naming everybody and I had zoned out on her, trying to figure out why he was talking to my baby. "Mommy, are you listening to me?"

"Yes, baby. When did he start coming to your school?"

"Today. When my teacher called my name, he said he knew a lot of Hendersons in Nome. When I told him who my daddy was, he said they went to school together and were friends. He's gonna be there helping out in the mornings and afternoons until his arm and ribs get better."

"What happened to him?" I asked.

I knew Karima was very inquisitive, so she probably asked him. "He said he got attacked by like five people at one time, but the police can't find them."

"Oh okay."

Karima kept talking as I headed to Sour Lake to get KJ. Karima's school was in a town called China, which was only a few minutes from Nome. The middle school KJ attended was in Sour Lake, which was also a few minutes from Nome, just in the opposite direction of China. As I drove, I tried to concentrate on the activities Kenny had planned for me. He'd been going out of his way to do nice things for me and had even taken me shoe shopping in Houston. These were things that we did all the time when we were married, so this was nothing new.

They'd broken ground at the store and his friend, Price was doing all the dirt work and Shylou had agreed to be a silent partner. That was what I loved about Kenny. His heart was huge. He could have bought Shylou out and had the business to himself, but he didn't mind helping others. Shylou had been a good friend to him as well. So, it was only right for Kenny to keep him from missing out on his money. When we got to the middle school, KJ was waiting for us. He got in the front seat and kissed me. That was unusual. I usually had to ask my seventh grader for a kiss. "Hey, Kendrall. How was school?"

"It was good. You looking at the future starting running back for the eighth grade team."

"Congratulations! That's awesome, baby!"

"I can't wait to show these white boys what it means to run a football."

I rolled my eyes. That Henderson cockiness didn't miss our son. Lord have mercy. When we got home, Kenny was standing outside, holding Kendrick, waiting on us to get there. Kendrick started clapping when we turned in the driveway. He was such a sweet baby. Tasha had gotten him a couple more times without drama or occurrences. He was even clean when she brought him back. Kenny always made sure he was here when she picked him up and dropped him home, so I wouldn't have to deal with her ass.

The kids hopped out the car as soon as I put it in park, running to their dad and Kendrick. Karima took him from Kenny and spun him around. KJ was a ball of excitement as he told his dad his good news. Once the kids had talked to Kenny and filled him in on their day, his eyes rested on me. A shiver made its way through my body. I couldn't help the smile that appeared on my face. That was the exact same way I felt when I saw him for the first time in that grocery store parking lot. "And how was your day, gorgeous?" he asked when I got closer to him.

"It was good, baby," I said, noticing the car parked off to the side. "Who's here?"

He pulled me in his arms and said, "Don't worry about all that. Just know that your man done hooked you up."

"Is that right?"

He kissed my lips, gently sucking the bottom one into his mouth. When his lips left mine, he said, "We'll be back in a couple of hours. Enjoy your time, baby. I love you."

"Thank you, Kenny. I love you, too."

I watched them get in his truck and leave, then walked in the house to find a massage table in the front room. "Hello, Mrs. Henderson. I'm Thalia and I'll be your masseuse for the evening."

"Wow. Thank you. Can I take a shower first?"

"Of course."

I looked around at the flowers strategically placed around the room and the platter of grapes, strawberries, cheese, and crackers. There was also a bottle of wine in a bucket of ice with a wine glass sitting next to it. Going up the stairs, I noticed there were flower petals leading the way to the bathroom. The smile that spread across my face had to be lighting up the entire house. Kenny made me so happy and I couldn't help but to thank God that he was willing to take me back after all the bullshit I'd put him through. The tears that filled my eyes came streaming down my face. They were tears of joy and gratefulness that the man I nearly destroyed was still here, showing me unconditional love. When I walked in the bathroom, there was already a bubble bath ran for me with flower petals in it. I took my phone from my pocket and took a picture. There was also a glass of wine next to the tub and soft music was playing.

Kenny was the real deal and so romantic. I'd heard his family say that he was a chip off the old block when he'd cheated. But that was far from the truth. His heart was pure. I'd sent him to the arms of another woman. Kenny wasn't that type of man. I'd forced him to become someone he wasn't. I quickly sent him a text that read, *This is beautiful. Thank you so much, baby.*

I disrobed as I listened to Vedo and sank my body in the tub of hot water. I knew I couldn't relax too long, since the lady was waiting for me downstairs. There was a robe hanging on the door for me to wear back downstairs. My phone chimed, alerting me of a text. I grabbed it to see Kenny had texted back. *Just something to show you how much I love and appreciate you. Although, that isn't enough to properly show you. I plan to show you soon.*

I had to be the most blessed woman in the world.

K 13 K

K enny

"I AIN'T TALKED TO THAT NIGGA SINCE THAT DAY I PUNCHED HIM in his shit."

"Me either. Has he talked to Pops?" I asked Storm.

"Nope."

"That nigga is crazy." Turning my attention back to KJ, I yelled, "He needs to be a lil lower to the ground, son. We gon' work on him." Looking back at Storm, I said, "I'm prolly gon' have to call Zay for a favor. This horse needs a little more training."

"You know that nigga deep in that rodeo shit with Red. It will definitely be a favor, 'cause he'll have to find the time. How you and Keisha doing?"

"Man, better than ever. It feels like it did when we first met, besides the kids of course. We still haven't had sex, but I want to so bad. I'm setting up something this weekend. Kendrick will be with

Tasha and I'm gon' ask mama if KJ and Karima can stay there Saturday night."

"I can't believe you held out. That would have been me and Aspen, I would have gotten at her shit by the second day."

"Lies. Had that been you and Aspen, y'all wouldn't be together."

"You know what? You right about that shit. Nigga you got a heart of gold... shiiid, that shit platinum. I don't know how you did that shit, but more power to you, bruh."

"Reggie's punk ass was talking to my baby."

Storm frowned as I turned back to watch KJ. "Karima? What the fuck?"

"He was at the school volunteering and heard a teacher call her by her full name. Telling her that he knew all of us. That's all he better be up to, or I'll put a bullet in his head next time. My wife is one thing, but my baby girl is another."

"I feel you on that, bruh. Well, I'ma holla. The twins been on one today. Having four kids in the house ain't no joke."

"Well, quit all that unprotected fucking."

Storm laughed loudly. "And yo' ass one to talk!"

"Yeah, but I ain't the one complaining about kids, either."

"Nigga, I ain't complaining. I'm just saying. Man, shut the fuck up. Why am I tryna explain shit to you? I'm out."

I shook my head slowly, then looked over at Karima and Kendrick playing in the hay. Keisha was quickly becoming my obsession again. While I still had some trust issues, they were dissipating more and more with each passing day. We'd had two counseling sessions and the counselor had observed what we knew all along. Our personalities were a lot alike. Usually in a marriage, one person was the talker and the other wasn't. But in our case, neither of us were talkers, nor were we confrontational. It took a lot for us to explode. However, verbalizing things we already knew about one another seemed to help remind us of why things went crazy. We needed to be reminded so we didn't repeat those behaviors. But it also reminded us of why we were perfect for one another.

The kids had done their homework and I'd taken them to Sonic to get something to eat. The food choices were slim in our area. I had to go to Sour Lake. There were only a couple of options there. Subway, Dairy Queen, pizza, or Sonic. That was it. "KJ! Let's wrap up. We'll come back tomorrow with Aunt Tiff. Maybe she can help you a little more."

"Okay."

After getting Kendrick and Karima out the hay, KJ had already stalled his horse. We visited with my parents for a little bit, then we headed home. They'd sent some stew home for us as well, so I didn't have to stop to get Keisha anything to eat. When we got there, the masseuse had just backed out the driveway. *Perfect timing.* I knew Keisha was feeling extremely relaxed, especially if she drank a lot of that wine. "A'ight. Y'all don't go in with a lot of noise. Your mom may be sleeping."

"Okay, Daddy," Karima said.

They went ahead inside while I got Kendrick out of his car seat. As I did, my phone rang. It was Tasha. I rolled my eyes to the sky, then answered. "Hello?"

"Hey, Kenny. I wanted to see if I could get Kendrick Thursday night instead of Friday. We're taking pictures Friday. That was the only day the photographer could get us in."

"Okay. That's fine. I'll have his things ready for the day after tomorrow, instead of Friday. I needed to verbalize that, so I won't forget."

"Okay. See y'all Thursday."

I ended the call and went inside the house to find Keisha on the couch knocked out. I smiled at her, then headed upstairs with Kendrick. Tasha had been on her grown woman shit... finally. She'd finally stopped giving me a hard time about Kendrick and was taking care of him like she should. She had even had a short conversation with Keisha. That shit was surprising as hell. So, I didn't have a problem letting him go a day early. After bringing him upstairs with KJ, I went back downstairs to get Keisha.

When I got down there, she was sitting on the sofa, looking disoriented. I chuckled, then made my way to her. "Hey, baby. You enjoy your massage?"

"Kenny, thank you so much. I more than enjoyed it."

"Why don't you go upstairs and lie down. Unless you wanna eat first. Mama sent you some stew."

"You know I love Mama Henderson's stew."

"Okay. I'll fix you some."

She stood from the couch and laid a kiss on me that almost had her face down ass up on that couch. I gently slid my hand over her cheek. She would be so shocked this weekend when I gave her all what we'd been dying to feel. I'd been celibate a long ass time, almost two years, and I couldn't wait to slide up in her gushy shit. Slowly stepping away from her, I asked, "Can you get Kendrick from KJ? He was waiting on me to come back and get him so he could take a shower.

"Yeah, sure."

I could see the desire in her eyes, and I couldn't wait to fulfill her every desire this weekend. After I fixed her food and had warmed it, she had sat at the bar. When I sat it in front of her with a side of potato salad, she licked her lips. While she was thinking about the food, I was imagining that tongue on my dick. This period in our lives had taught me the importance of intimacy, though. As she ate, my phone rang. I lifted my eyes to the sky when I saw Storm's name. "Hello?"

"What are y'all doing tomorrow evening?"

"Not too much. Why?"

"Aspen wanted me to invite y'all to dinner."

"Is WJ gonna be there?"

"Hell naw. You know I ain't fucking with that nigga right now. Just Jasper and Tiff and their families. Jenahra and Chrissy said they didn't know if they were coming or not because it was a weekday. They can stay their bougie asses at home. That'll be fine by me. Mama and Daddy coming, too."

"Okay. Well, we'll be there. What time?"

"Six."

"Okay. See y'all then."

After ending the call, I looked over at Keisha, stuffing her face. I chuckled as I watched her. "Kenny, I was hungry!"

She slapped my arm, causing me to laugh more. "We're invited to dinner tomorrow night at Storm's."

"Okay."

"I'm gonna go bathe Kendrick and get him ready for bed. He's tired."

"I can tell. He's been extremely quiet."

"Yeah. You think you'll be able to braid my hair tonight?"

"Of course."

After leaning in to kiss me, she continued eating her dinner. I couldn't wait to sit between those thighs and imagine I was doing more than sitting between them.

❦

"First of all, you can miss me with that shit! Ain't nothing soft about none of this shit. Ask Aspen."

We all laughed as Aspen put her hand to her face. I didn't know how she dealt with Storm on an everyday basis. Aspen had cooked a seafood feast: fried fish, shrimp etouffee, barbeque crabs, hush puppies, and French fries. There was salad and corn on the cob as well. We'd eaten until we were full and were now having a good time in his family room. Storm had pulled Aspen's feet to his lap and was massaging them when Jasper called him soft. "Secondly, I know yo' ass do shit like that with Chas, plus some. I won't say what that plus some is since Mama and Daddy here."

Jasper turned red as hell, which really made us crack up. Tiff was holding her little pouch as she laughed. She was so cute pregnant. I couldn't believe baby sis was married and pregnant. She was always so independent. Not long after the shenanigans, Mama and Daddy

113

had enough and decided to go home. When they did, Jasper pulled a blunt from his pocket. "Who rolling outside with me?"

Me, Ryder and Storm all stood and headed outside. Although Storm and I weren't really smokers, I'd probably take a pull from it tonight. My dick had been hard all day. This weekend couldn't get here fast enough. When she'd braided my hair last night and I felt the heat coming from that thang between her legs, I nearly lost it. Every day got harder and harder to restrain, but I wanted our first time in almost two years to be unrestricted. We could fuck all over the house and be as loud as we wanted to be if the kids weren't home. Saturday was gonna be our day. But shit, we would probably start Friday night.

Jasper fired up the blunt and took the first pull, then passed it to Ryder. "So, I saw Reggie earlier today," Jasper said. "That nigga looked at me, then hurriedly got the fuck out of my way. He looked scared as shit, so I don't think we'll have any more problems with his punk ass."

We all laughed. "Well, that's good to hear, since he was talking to my baby at school."

"I think he was just looking for a way to get under your skin. That muthafucka ain't gon' do nothing. He can't risk losing his job any more than he already has. That shit he did with Keisha could get him fired and he knows that. If he would have pressed charges on us, all that shit would have come out," Ryder said, enlightening us.

"You must have done your research, bruh. Good looking out," Jasper said.

Storm had taken a pull from the ganja and passed it to me. After taking a pull, I said, "You know what we haven't done in a while?"

"What?" they all asked in unison.

"Had our daddy daughter day."

"I know, it's been a minute," Storm added.

"I can't wait to see if Tiff's having a boy or girl. It doesn't matter what we have, but I can't wait to know."

"Y'all gon' have a girl. Watch," Storm said.

"I think it's gon' be a boy. How far along is she again?" I asked.

"She's only fifteen weeks. I feel like I'm 'bout to lose it. We ain't even halfway there and lil baby already on one, tryna boss up on a nigga all the damn time. I just bite the fuck outta my tongue and do what she demands. She better be glad she pregnant."

We all laughed as he took an extra-long pull off the blunt. "Tiff already bossy anyway, so I can imagine," Jasper said.

"So, what we gon' do about WJ ass?"

"Make sure he out of the loop on every fucking thing and I've already told Chasity, Tiff, and Mama not to give him any fucking information about what we got going on in the business office. Everybody knows to shut that nigga out of business. The only thing he's gonna be tending to is his tractor shop. That's it. We gotta get at Marcus, too," Jasper said.

"Ooooh, let me get at Marcus. Ain't nobody gon' do that shit like me," Storm said.

I laughed, because Storm had to be the rudest of all of us. It came so natural for him to be that way. The rest of us had to be pushed. That nigga was just rude for no reason. "Man, have at it, bruh," Jasper said. "But we gon' approach his bitch-ass together, too."

"Yeah. He needs to know that we'll all fuck him up," I added.

When we finished smoking, we all headed back in the house. I walked over to Keisha and kissed her lips. "You ready to go? We need to get the kids in the bed."

"Yeah, we do. I'm ready."

I called for the kids and told everybody goodnight, then thanked Aspen and Storm for the meal. When we got home, I was feeling slightly high. Once the kids went to bed and Keisha had gotten out of the shower, I wanted to dig up in her even more so than before we left to head to Storm's house. I wrapped my arms around her waist from behind and kissed her neck. "Mmm, you smell good, baby."

She giggled and turned around in my arms. "I would hate to take advantage of how high you are right now. Have you regretting shit tomorrow."

"Maaaan, you could just go with the flow and fuck how I'm gon' feel about the shit tomorrow," I said, then bit her earlobe.

She moaned as her hands went to the back of my head. "I love you, Kenny, but I'm gonna wait. Had this not been our first time back in the saddle, I would've ridden you into the sunset."

I chuckled at her country inuendo, then pulled away from her, visualizing all the shit I would be doing to her beautiful body this weekend. "Okay, baby. I love you, too."

I followed her to the room she was sleeping in and kissed her lips passionately, moving to her neck. Pulling her into me, I slid my hands to her ass while she moaned. "Damn, Keisha. You so fucking fine. I can't seem to help myself."

"You fine as hell, too, Kenny, but we have to wait until you're clear-headed."

"I know," I whispered against her ear. I kissed it, then said, "Goodnight, baby."

"Goodnight."

Letting her go, I walked down the hall to my room, fully prepared to jack off to visions of her naked body and how pleased I would have been to touch her insides.

❧ 14 ❧

K eisha

WHEN KENNY GOT HOME FROM BRINGING THE KIDS TO HIS parents' house, I was in the mirror primping, making sure I looked so sexy for him, until he wouldn't be able to resist filling me with that Henderson beef. God, I was suffering in silence. It had been over a month and I hadn't felt him inside of me yet. I was doing my best to be patient, but I felt like tonight had to be the night. I couldn't sleep in his room every night, because I would have taken him down by now. Sucking him off in his sleep, then hopped on that dick so fast, until he wouldn't be able to stop me.

He told me to get dressed in something nice, but not too dressy. I wasn't exactly sure where we were going, but I was never disappointed wherever Kenny took me or what he surprised me with. Paying great attention to detail, he always knew what I would love. So, I put on some black tights, a fitted, graphic tee and some black heels. I'd pulled my dreads up and styled them in a way I knew he would like, then applied my makeup. Once I finished primping, I put on my jewelry and headed down the stairs to find him at the bottom of them, waiting for me.

Kenny looked amazing in his black jeans, Henderson tee, and white forces. He'd taken his hair loose and I just wanted to grab handfuls of it while he made love to me. Extending his arm, he handed me a bouquet of calla lilies. I smiled brightly and kissed his cheek. "Thank you, baby."

He smiled at me, giving me all the damn feels. Goosebumps had invaded my flesh just from looking at all that man in front of me. From his hair to his beard screamed sex appeal. From looking at him, I would have never guessed he was a country boy. Those diamond studs and hair would have never been associated with him riding a horse. After going to the kitchen and putting my flowers in water, I turned back to him. The look in his eyes was so serious, I didn't know what to make of it. When I got close to him, he grabbed my hand and pulled me to him. "Damn, baby. You look so good. You *always* look good."

"You always look good, too, baby. I almost want to stay home."

"We won't be gone long."

Was he saying that I was gonna get what I was insinuating? Instead of asking, I went with the flow and smiled at him. Sliding his fingers down the side of my face to my arm and back to my hand, he led me to the door and out of it to a beautiful, white Rolls Royce Phantom. I turned back to look at him with wide eyes. "Kenny! Is that the same car?"

"Hell yeah."

I jumped into his arms and he spun me around. When we'd gotten married and were going home from our honeymoon suite, we'd seen this car. I'd told him that one day I would love to just ride in a car like that. I didn't have to own one, but I wanted to ride in luxury like that. And here we were, almost fourteen years later. He still remembered. I left his arms and ran to the car while he laughed at me. The driver got out and opened the door for me and I stood there in awe. Kenny put his hand at the small of my back and asked, "You gon' get in, babe?"

I slowly sat in the seat and slid to the other side as he got in as well. When the driver closed the door, I nearly tackled Kenny's ass. My lips landed on his and I kissed him deeply while bringing my palm to his face. Quickly pulling away, I looked around at the inside of the car and squealed in excitement. We didn't have to do anything else, because this shit took the cake. However, we ended up at The Grill and I noticed no one else was there. He'd rented out the entire restaurant and had an amazing band there, playing live jazz music. I'd eaten as much lamb as my stomach could take and he'd eaten the porterhouse chop.

Once we left, he took me to the riverfront to walk and talk for a bit. Hand in hand, we enjoyed the sound of the water. "Keisha, this thing between us has been going so well. I'm trusting you more and more every day. This feels like old times, when we were dating. It feels like we're practically dating again. I did all this tonight to tell you and show you how much I love you and how much I want you. Tonight, I wanna go places with you that I have only imagined for the past couple of years. I wanna make love to you."

I stopped walking and looked into his eyes to see how serious he was. The tears escaped my eyes, but they were tears of happiness. He gently swiped them away, and said, "One day soon, you gon' be my wife again."

I pulled his face to mine and kissed him hungrily, trying to nourish my soul with the heart that was pouring into me through his tongue. There was no other place I would rather be than in his arms. Despite the past hurts and betrayals we'd suffered at the hands of one another, we somehow had made it through. He pulled away from me and said, "Let's get the fuck outta here and get home."

I hopped in excitement as he chuckled. Making it to the car in mere seconds, I practically dove across the seat. My shit was pulsating, waiting to feel his touch and his kisses. Whenever he used to eat me out, he would slowly kiss on it, like he loved her more than me. We touched on one another and kissed the entire way to Nome, and thankfully, it didn't seem like it had taken twenty minutes to get here. Once the driver got to the house and had opened the door, I quickly made my way to the porch, because the rain had started falling.

Kenny stood there, getting soaked as the car backed away and I couldn't help but smile. We used to always fantasize about making love in the rain, but we'd never done it. He pulled his shirt off with his bottom lip tucked in his mouth, then gestured with his head for me to follow him to the other side of the house. Taking off my heels on the porch, I did just that. I walked out in that rain, to get my man. As soon as I rounded the corner of the house, he was there, pulling me into his arms. Quickly pulling my shirt over my head, Kenny's lips found mine as he unfastened my bra. When it fell to the ground, he immediately went to my nipples, sucking the fuck out of them.

Turning me to where my back was against the house, he swiftly unbuttoned my pants and helped me shimmy out of them. Once I did, he turned me around, my back to him and caressed my breasts, fondling the rings that slightly hung from my nipples. God, it felt like I was leaking down my legs. This had been a long time coming and we didn't rush to get here. When I felt his dick breach my opening, I could have screamed. "Kenny! Oh my God!"

His dick was so good, it was no wonder I was fiending for it. It had a slight hook in that shit that hit my G-spot every time. As he stroked me, I cried out, knowing he wouldn't be able to see my tears in this rain. The sensations I was feeling had to be supernatural. "Kenny! I'm cumming, baby! Shit!"

"Yeah, give me that shit, baby."

He was always so fucking smooth. I loved his ass. Looking back at him, his curly hair was hanging down his back. His lips met mine and we kissed as we made love right there outside against the side of the fucking house. Sliding out of me, he turned me around and lifted me, sliding me down his dick. I wrapped my legs around him and held his head close to me as my legs trembled. Lowering my head to his lips as he gripped my ass, I kissed him, licking at his bottom lip and sucking it. He began slamming me on his dick and I couldn't take it. I was cumming again. As I closed my eyes, Kenny said, "Naw. Keep them open, Keisha. Look at me while you cum. Let me see how much you fucking love this shit."

I wanted to scream, but we lived too close to Tiff. I couldn't have her coming down here, catching us fucking. "Kenny! Shit!"

His phone started ringing in his pocket, causing him to slow his stroke. Choosing to ignore it, he kept stroking me, but it rang again. "Shit!"

He lowered me to my feet and said, "Let's go in the house, baby."

We ran to the porch like horny teenagers who didn't want to get caught. When he opened the door, we dropped our wet things right there on the tile, then he got his phone from his pocket. Good thing that shit was waterproof. He frowned at the number just as it began ringing again. "Hello?" he answered somewhat winded.

His face frowned up even more, then he yelled, "Hell naw! Where? Where is he?!"

My eyes watered as I searched his for a clue of what was going on while shivering from the cold. "Fuck! I'm on my way. Who do I need to ask for when I get there?"

The tears were now streaming down his face and I couldn't stop them from falling down my cheeks, either. He ended the call, then ran to the kitchen and threw up in the sink. I ran to him, putting my hand on his back, feeling his wet skin. "Kenny, what's wrong?"

"Kendrick's in ICU and they don't think he's gonna make it. Tasha has been arrested. We gotta get to Houston. Shit! I can't lose my son! Fuck!" he screamed.

He finished undressing right there at the sink and I followed him upstairs to get dressed. There was no time for showers. We just had to dry off as best we could and put on dry clothes. My mind was everywhere, trying to figure out why that baby was in ICU. What had Tasha done? God! Throwing on some sweats and a t-shirt, I slid my tennis shoes on and grabbed a pair of socks to put on in the car.

Running down the stairs behind him, I slammed the door, not even bothering to lock it. When we got in and he had backed out, getting to Highway 90, I asked, "Kenny what happened?"

"The neighbor heard Kendrick screaming for an extended amount of time, so they went to see what was going on. She had beaten my son and poured bleach in his mouth. That bitch! That fucking bitch!"

The tears were pouring from my face. After putting my socks and shoes on, I grabbed his hand. "Kenny, pull over and let me drive."

"No! That's gon' waste too much time. We may not have time! My son may not make it!"

I didn't know how he could see the road with all the tears that were falling from his eyes. I got my phone from my purse and called Mom and Dad Henderson and asked them to alert the family. Just when it seemed everything was going well, this had to happen. Tasha deserved to get fucked up. Somebody needed to pour bleach down her fucking throat. People didn't usually survive bleach ingestion. That baby had suffered. That shit had to have eaten his insides, igniting it on fire and there was nothing he could do to stop it.

As he continued to drive, we both cried audibly. I didn't know how to soothe his heart, because mine was hurting, too. I'd come to fall in love with that little boy like he was mine. While I never fell in love with the idea of Tasha being around, that baby didn't have a choice in the matter. He was brought here by their lust. Kendrick was easy to fall in love with, and the closer we got to the hospital, the more my heart crumbled. I didn't know what condition he would be in when we got there or how much bleach he'd ingested. *Jesus help us.*

My phone started ringing and it was Storm. He never really called me, but he probably knew that Kenny was inconsolable right now. "Hello?"

"I need to know where that bitch at and what hospital. We're on our way."

"Methodist in Houston. Tasha has been arrested already."

"That lucky bitch. I'd never put my hands on a woman, but I was prepared to go to jail for fucking her up. How close are y'all?"

"We're about fifteen minutes away."

"We're hitting the road now. Everybody is following us, and Mama and Daddy have all the kids."

"O-okay. Thanks."

He ended the call. His entire family was coming to support him, and I was grateful for that.

When we got to the hospital, we didn't really know where to go, so I told him the emergency room should be able to tell us something, since that was where he came through. The tears were still streaming down our faces and the tremble in Kenny's body had almost crippled me. Once he gave the lady at the desk the name of the lady that called him, someone came from the back and led us to where we needed to be.

When we approached the desk, the lady brought us to a consultation room. I didn't think this was a good sign. As we sat, Kenny looked over at me. The emotion and turmoil in his eyes was too much to bear, but I did my best to try to carry it all. Slowly rubbing his hand between mine, I whispered, "I'm here for you, baby."

No sooner than I did, a doctor came in with a solemn look on his face. We stood to our feet, and as the doctor extended his hand to shake Kenny's, he yelled, "No! Tell me my son is alright. Tell me he's gonna be okay."

The doctor lowered his head and began, "He ingested too much. It burned tissue in his mouth, esophagus, and stomach. His blood pressure was extremely low, and he was unconscious when they got here. The ambulance immediately gave him water, but it was too late. We're basically keeping him alive just so you can see him, but the minute we remove the life support and blood pressure medicine, he's going to let go. I'm so sorry."

Kenny fell to the floor and I fell to my knees with him. Wrapping my arms around him as he fell apart was so hard. I'd never seen

Kenny like this, and it was tearing me apart as well. "She killed my baby, Keisha. What am I gonna do without my son?"

"Come on, baby. Let's go see him."

We both stood to our feet and followed the doctor to his room in ICU. Kenny ran to his side and broke down even more so when he saw him. The burns around his mouth and just the condition of his mouth, let us know just how cruel Tasha had been. There was no telling how long it had been before the neighbor had heard his screams. I couldn't take it. Kenny was practically lying on his body, begging him not to leave him. I did my best to pray, but I was too angry and hurt to get a word out. Wrapping my arms around Kenny's waist and laying my head against him, brought him back to me.

He stood up straight, then nodded at the nurse and doctors that had gathered in the room. The moment they disconnected the tubes, Kendrick was gone. As we stood there in the room, crying our eyes out, I felt arms around us. All his brothers and sisters had arrived, with the exception of WJ. There wasn't a dry eye in the room. Once the funeral home was called, they allowed us to go back to the consultation room, but Kenny refused. He wanted to sit with Kendrick. So, that was where I would be as well.

15

K enny

STARING AT MY DEAD SON ONLY CAUSED MY HEART TO BURN. I
had to be living in a horrible nightmare that I couldn't wake up from.
I would have never thought Tasha was capable of this. Not in a
million years. *How could she do this to an innocent child?* She had
been doing well with him, making me let down my guard concerning
her. Kendrick had gotten to where he was excited to see her and that
had made my heart happy. But this? This was unthinkable. Only a
devil could do something like this. I'd come to the conclusion that I
had slept with the devil. There was no way I would have relin-
quished him to her, knowing she could do something so vile and evil.

I was in a trance-like state as my son lay in that bed. Standing
from my chair and releasing Keisha's hand, I got in bed with him.
The overwhelming scent of bleach invaded my nostrils and it
produced tears I thought I no longer had, to stream down my face.

Pulling his lifeless body in my arms, I couldn't help but crumble. "Kendrick, Daddy's so sorry. I'm so sorry, son. You suffered so much."

I rocked back and forth as I held him in my arms, like I used to do when he first started living with me. "God, I'm sorry."

Keisha had come to the side of the bed and rubbed my head as I kissed my son repeatedly. How I would move on from this was a mystery, and at the moment, I didn't want to move on. The weight of this was suffocating me. I shouldn't have trusted her to take him. The court orders were for her to get him every two weeks. If she didn't want him, she didn't have to come get him. No one was forcing her to take him. The more I thought about Tasha, the angrier I got. I was grateful that she was already locked up, because I would have killed her... choked her ass to death.

Before long, the funeral home had arrived to take his body. I had never heard of them, but they came highly recommended from the hospital staff. I would have to get his body transported to Beaumont to have his funeral. I stood from the bed and walked out to the hallway while they handled their business. Keisha wrapped her arms around my waist, but right now, I couldn't feel her love or her support. I felt numb. I wanted to remain that way, because maybe the loss of my son... my baby, wouldn't hurt as bad.

My family came out of the consultation room and surrounded us as the funeral home prepared to take my son. They knew I would need as much support as possible. Sure enough, when they wheeled Kendrick out of the room in that black bag, I almost lost it. My brothers were able to restrain me, keeping me from tearing shit up in the hospital. The funeral director was talking to Keisha as I tried to calm down. My fucking son was dead. I jerked away from my brothers and went to Keisha as the funeral director was walking off. "What he say?"

"For you to call when you're ready to make arrangements. I'm so sorry, baby."

I pulled her in my arms as she cried, knowing we had a long road ahead of us. How would I recover from this? Death was something I wasn't expecting to experience any time soon, especially not one of my children. I needed to know why she did it. Although no excuse was acceptable, I needed to know why. When I let Keisha go, I grabbed her hand and we walked out of the ICU unit, my family behind us. "Kenny, let me drive y'all home," Tiffany said.

I handed her the keys without a fight, because I was in no condition to drive. Neither of us were. As we continued to an elevator, Jasper said, "Mama went to your house with KJ and Karima, so they could make sure things were in order. She's gonna stay overnight. We will all be there tomorrow to cook and do whatever else y'all need us to do. Most of all to keep y'all company."

I nodded in acceptance. It didn't matter what they did. I wanted my son back and no one could give me that. Once outside, everyone hugged me, assuring me that they would be at the house tomorrow. Then Tiffany walked with us to the emergency room parking to drive us back. No words were spoken, just tears falling down our cheeks. Keisha and I got in the backseat and Tiff drove us back to Nome with Ryder right behind us.

After walking inside, I immediately walked up the stairs as my mama tried to talk to me. I couldn't talk right now. Keisha stayed downstairs with her as I made my way to Kendrick's room. After closing the door, I went to my knees and cried out to God. "Why? Why did you let this happen? After allowing her to conceive and giving me full custody of him, why would you allow him to be taken from me? I know you're God and you don't owe us a thing, but I'm trying to understand. Right now I feel lost, stumbling through here without direction. All I can think about is how happy Kendrick had been, especially since Keisha, KJ, and Karima had been here. I don't know what to do. All I feel is sadness and rage. I need you."

After lying in Kendrick's bed, I stared at the ceiling, holding his favorite teddy bear that Mama had bought him. The tears wouldn't stop. I sat up and slid to the floor, looking at all the toys I'd tried to spoil him with and how he'd rather play with the boxes they came in. He loved Paw Patrol, and just like Karima loved for me to sing "Rock with You" to her, he loved for me to sing "Billie Jean" ironically. I rubbed my hands down my face, trying to come to grips with the fact that I would never see him again. He wouldn't be here for me to tell to stop meddling in the cabinets or stop pulling clothes out of the drawers.

No one would be sitting on my shoulders or playing in the hay while I worked outside... or rather trying to eat the hay. Who would I pull around in that toy tractor? Anytime I made spaghetti, he looked like a giant meatball when he finished. Then I'd tickle him until he could barely breathe and clean him up. I'd just started getting used to his hugs and him yelling Da-Da. I broke down, sitting on the floor and cried audibly. "God! Why my son?"

As I cried, I heard a soft knock on the door, then Keisha walked in. She came and sat on the floor next to me, grabbing my hand. "Baby, being in this room probably isn't the best thing right now. Come with me and take a shower, then we'll go to the room."

I nodded, then stood from the floor, helping her up as well. My emotions were going haywire, and I didn't know how to control them right now. When we walked in the bedroom, I stripped as Keisha started the shower. Looking in the mirror at my hair, I knew I would have to wash it. All I had the energy to do was walk to the bed to fall in it. When Keisha came back, she was naked. Grabbing me by the hand, she led me to the shower and once we were in, the hot water soaked us. As it loosened my muscles, I closed my eyes. The hot water was doing its job. When I felt Keisha's hands on me, I opened my eyes to stare into hers. She was washing my body and I was grateful. However, I knew she was hurting, too. She'd treated Kendrick like he was her son, letting me know how serious she was about being in my life again.

Kendrick was a daily reminder that I'd been fucking Tasha, but she accepted him into her life without the least complaint. He'd even started calling her Ma-Ma, mimicking Karima and KJ. I backed under the spray and she grabbed the shampoo. Gently taking it from her hand, I put it down and began washing her body. At that moment, it was like God spoke to me. *Your love for each other will get you through this difficult time.*

She moaned softly as I applied pressure to her shoulders and slid the loofah down her back. When I did, I softly kissed her neck and whispered in her ear, "Thank you for tending to me when you need tending to as well."

A soft whimper left her, and I continued washing her body, then rinsed her off. I washed my hair and she did the same, since our festivities from earlier had left us both looking like wet dogs. After we'd washed the shampoo out and had conditioned, I stared at her and gave her a weak smile, hoping that she could see that she was my comfort. Lowering my lips to hers, I sought solace in her love and the way she kissed me back, she sought it in me, too. Without giving it another thought, I picked her up and slid her down my dick.

While my heart was hurting, I still needed to feel that love that I only got from within her walls. Her love was like the peace that surpassed all understanding. Making love to her put my soul at ease. She grabbed handfuls of my hair as the tears streamed down her face and held on tightly. Her expressions only mirrored mine, because I couldn't stop the tears, even now. My cries were escaping me as I dug into her, pouring the love I had in my heart for Kendrick into her. She slid down my body and we embraced one another, both crying uncontrollably.

⌘

"KENNY USED TO THINK HE WAS THE ONLY ONE THAT KNEW HOW to cut around here. Talking 'bout, *move Jasper. Let me handle this shit.* I mean, I'll give it to him, the nigga was good at it, but shit, we all knew how to do it. It just took us all a little longer," Jasper joked, trying to keep our minds off of last night.

My family had all come over and had been here since breakfast. Jenahra was cooking lunch and Chrissy and Tiffany would be cooking dinner. Mama had cooked breakfast. Jasper and Storm had done their best to keep the mood light as I sat quietly on the couch, occasionally smiling at their stories and jokes. Hearing the laughter around me was making things easier to deal with. Keisha had stayed tucked under me all day. The kids were devastated when we told them the news this morning and it took a lot out of me to verbalize it. That only reminded me that this tragedy had indeed happened. It wasn't a nightmare.

We'd all cried together, and I promised them that I wouldn't check out on them. Karima almost took me out, though, when she'd asked if she was gonna die, too. That caused me to break down all over again. We should have been planning her seventh birthday party, but we were planning my one-year-old son's funeral. I'd called the funeral home and we'd decided to just go with a gravesite service. I didn't know any of Tasha's family and I didn't care to know them.

A detective from Liberty County had already called as well and had talked to me about the information they'd gotten from the neighbor. They would be making a visit to us within the next couple of days as well. When the doorbell rang, Storm hopped up to go answer it and came back with WJ and his family. Everyone in the room got quiet as hell. His two youngest daughters took off to go find Karima and he and Sharon stood there awkwardly. Finally, Sharon cleared her throat and began speaking to everybody as WJ approached me. "I know we need to talk about a lot, but I couldn't not come and offer my condolences for Kendrick."

I stood and shook his hand as I nodded. Once upon a time, he and I were closer than I was to Jasper. Jasper was three years younger than me, but WJ was the one that showed me how to do things around the farm. I had always looked up to him as a kid. He was six years older than me and was everything I thought I wanted to be growing up. When I sat back down, I noticed everyone staring at him. He looked around uncomfortably, then cleared his throat. "I owe everyone an apology, especially you, Dad."

Storm rolled his eyes and Jasper looked the opposite direction. Tiffany had a deep frown on her face. *Those youngest three stooges.*

They had the worst tempers out of the seven of us and caught the most whippings growing up for always getting into mischief. WJ continued, "It was nothing you could change. I was angry about the situation with Marcus as all of us were. Even though we talked, I can't say that I released forgiveness. My issue wasn't with the fact that Marcus was even created. I was pissed that you hid him and didn't claim him as your son. I think that bothered us all as well. It's no excuse for what I did, but I knew I needed to explain."

"Well, that explanation weak as hell. That's some feminine bullshit if I ever heard it," Storm said.

Surprisingly, WJ didn't respond to him. His eyes remained on Pop. "Dad, please forgive me. I'm not asking for you to ever trust me again, because I don't deserve your trust. But I know I won't be able to go through the rest of my life without having your forgiveness. You probably can't believe that I have the audacity to ask for that after what I did, but I don't have anything to lose by begging that you forgive me."

He lowered his head as Dad stood to his feet. "Wesley, I know you like the back of my own head. I'll forgive you, when you tell me the truth."

WJ's eyes met his as he said, "I was being greedy and underhanded, knowing that you were at the point of retirement anyway, I figured you wouldn't notice. Instead of waiting for my time, I wanted it now. I solicited Marcus to help me, offering him a cut. It wasn't his idea, but he went along with it, knowing that it would possibly benefit him. I apologize to all of you. I'm supposed to love and protect my family, but instead I betrayed your trust."

"Now, that was the truth. I forgive you, WJ, but it's gonna take some time for me to trust you... if ever, son. What you were trying to do could have bankrupt us. Your siblings would have never forgiven you."

"I don't forgive his punk ass now," Storm blurted, then walked out the house with Jasper on his trail.

I didn't have the energy to even add to the conversation because at this point, I didn't give a shit about none of that stuff. Pulling Keisha closer to me, I kissed her forehead as Pop hugged WJ. When they separated, WJ said, "I'm gonna go. I'll see you guys later."

He went to the kitchen and kissed Sharon, leaving her and the kids here. Jenahra came out the kitchen and said, "The potato soup is ready."

"'Bout time. I'm hungry as hell," Tiff said as Ryder rubbed her belly.

I swallowed hard, because Kendrick always came to mind when I looked at her stomach. I wanted this to just be over. Storm and Jasper came back inside, and Jasper went straight to the kitchen and came back with a bowl and handed it to me. I didn't want to eat, but I knew I had to. Keisha sat up and after we blessed the food, I served her the first spoon. "It's really good, Jenahra," Keisha said as Jenahra served Mama and Daddy.

"Thank you, Keisha."

I sat there and fed the both of us from that one bowl until we were done. But suddenly a wave of nausea hit me. I sprang from the couch as images of my son's deformed mouth sprinted through my mind, running to the bathroom. Regurgitating my insides in the toilet, my cries for my son escaped me. That was the very reason we were having a gravesite service. I couldn't bear to see him that way again and I didn't want anyone else to see him that way, especially KJ and Karima. As I flushed the toilet, Keisha was at the sink with some mouthwash and a wet towel. After rinsing my mouth, she gently washed my face. "We're gonna make it through this, baby."

I nodded as I stared in her eyes. The love we made last night had taken over my thoughts. It was passionate and emotional. After we'd gotten out of the shower, I made love to her again, not being able to contain myself. I'd missed how she felt, and part of the reason for waiting as long as I did was for her last sexual episode with her ex-boyfriend to be out of her head. Since she'd been here, she never mentioned his name. As I was about to kiss her, I heard Storm's loud ass. Leaving the restroom, I heard him say, "Brothers don't do the fuck shit to each other that he did. He ain't my damn brother."

When I walked in the front room, Storm was standing on his feet, arguing with Jenahra. "You will not talk to me like that Storm. I deserve more respect from you than that."

"Well, respect my damn opinion and quit talking to me like a child. I'ma grown ass man with a wife and four kids."

When he looked up at me, his face turned red. "I'm sorry, Kenny. The last thing you need at your house is confusion."

He walked over to Aspen and apologized to her, too, because she was crying. "I'm sorry, baby. I'm gonna go home. Okay? You and the kids coming?"

"Yeah," she said as he wiped away her tears.

I took a deep breath, then sat on the couch. Jasper sat next to me and asked, "You wanna come to the shop, so I can edge you up?"

"I'll come Tuesday. I don't feel like talking to nobody and I know the shop is full."

"Well, I'll go get my clippers and come back to do it outside here. KJ needs an edge, too. It was y'all appointment day."

"Thanks, Jasper."

Once Storm and his family left, Jenahra said, "Storm really needs to grow up. WJ is our brother, regardless of what was done."

"Have you reminded WJ that we're his siblings? Especially when he thought it was okay to flirt with my wife. He gets a pass and we're supposed to accept his apology and move on like nothing ever happened, right, Jenahra?"

"I talked to WJ, Kenny. He didn't get a pass. What he did was wrong, and I haven't figured out what has gotten into him lately. But we can't fight fire with fire. That's all I'm saying, brother. I love all of you and I want to see us get along as a family. We're Hendersons. Doesn't that stand for something?"

I didn't justify her with an answer. She may have been right, but because WJ was blood, his actions hurt even more so. Had he not been, he would have gotten fucked up like Reggie's ass. She came and sat next to me and pulled me in her arms. "Hurt has had your address for the past few years, baby. I'm so sorry. You know you were always my baby."

Keisha's eyebrows had risen and so had mine. How did she know about the last *few* years? Had she said the last couple of years, I wouldn't have thought a thing about it. "What do you mean the last *few* years, Jenahra?"

"Umm... WJ told me everything when Keisha first came back."

"Everything like what?" Tiffany asked.

I lowered my head for a moment. "Can y'all just go home?"

"What about dinner, Kenny?" Chrissy asked.

Keisha stood and left the room. I knew she was embarrassed, but what could I do about it? If Jenahra knew, then I knew Chrissy knew. "I'm not worried about dinner, sis. Thank y'all for everything."

Chasity had stayed seated, because she was waiting for Jasper to come back, but Jenahra and Chrissy packed up, along with Mama and Daddy. Tiffany was sitting there with her legs crossed like she had no intentions on leaving. I didn't need this shit today. She finally stood from her seat as Ryder pulled her up. "I know now isn't a good time. But is it something I don't already know?"

Tiffany only knew about the shit that I did. I only told her that Keisha was holding out on me. I didn't want to cause confusion between her and Keisha, but it seemed she was gonna find out anyway. I couldn't look at her. Besides, I needed to go check on Keisha. Standing from my seat, Tiffany nodded, realizing that I couldn't answer her question. She walked over to me and hugged me, then whispered in my ear, "What's in the past doesn't matter, okay? Even if you think it may hurt me. I love you, Kenny, and I know it has to involve me in some way, because we talk about everything. Don't worry."

She kissed my cheek and I said in her ear, "I love you, too, sis. You and Ryder are welcomed to come back later after Jenahra and Chrissy leave."

She smiled at me, then left. Once everyone was gone, I looked over at Chasity and said, "Let me go check on Keisha right quick."

"It's okay, Kenny. Jasper should be back in a little bit."

I nodded at her, then went upstairs to find Keisha sitting on the floor in the room Mama had slept in. "Baby, you okay?"

"Tiffany is going to hate me."

"No, she won't. She has Ryder. I'll talk to her soon, because she isn't going to let me forget. Come back downstairs, baby. Everyone's gone except for Chasity."

"Okay."

We went back downstairs to find Jasper standing there with his clippers. KJ had been in his room all day. So, I went back up to get him so he could get an edge up. He was growing his hair out like mine. "Come on, son. Uncle Jasper is here to give us an edge."

"Okay. It feels weird not having to tell Kendrick to stop trying to eat my game controllers. That happened almost every day."

"Yeah. It's gonna feel weird around here for a while without him."

"Dad, it's okay to be weak in front of me. We all have weak moments."

"I know, son. Thanks."

And just like that, the tears fell from my eyes and my son shook my hand then hugged me. Love was going to get us through, but I wished it would hurry up.

❧ 16 ❧

K eisha

THINGS HAD BEEN QUIET AROUND THE HOUSE. AFTER JASPER
had edged up Kenny and KJ, Chasity started dinner. Tiffany and
Ryder came back, since they only lived a couple of houses down. She
was quieter than normal, though, and I knew it was because of what
she was trying to figure out. I did my best to keep the conversation on
her pregnancy, but it was hard. Instead of letting Kenny handle all
the pressure of his family, I decided to call Tiffany and ask her to
come over. I had the unmitigated gall to tell her about Kenny's shit, so
I needed to tell her about the shit I did. The kids had gone to school
and Kenny was at the store with Shylou and Price.

There was no better time than for me to suffer the consequences
of the wrath Tiffany would feel towards me. When the doorbell rang,
a tremble went through my body to my damn soul as I went to the
door. As I opened it, I could see the smile on her face. "Hey, Tiff."

"Hey, Keisha."

"Come on in. You want something to drink or eat?"

"No, I'm okay. Just a little nervous."

"Yeah, me too. Have a seat."

She went to the couch and sat as my phone rang. When I pulled it from my pocket, I saw it was Kenny. "Hello?"

"Hey, baby. I'm just checking on you. You okay?"

"Hey, Kenny. I'm okay, baby."

"Okay. I should be home within the next hour."

"Okay."

He ended the call. Yesterday when he'd left to go to Storm's house, he did the same thing. Always checking on me to make sure I was okay. That's how things were when we first got married. He was such a sweetheart. Although, I was far from okay at this moment. My stomach was in knots as I sat across from Tiff. She smiled at me as she rested her hand on her belly. "Tiff, first I need to apologize to you. Before I left for San Antonio, I ran Kenny down like a dog. That's your brother and I had no right."

"What do you mean? With all the shit you told me, I didn't blame you one bit."

"Kenny didn't destroy our marriage on his own. After I had Karima and after my six-weeks exam, I still wouldn't have sex with him, and it had nothing to do with him cheating. He hadn't cheated on me at that point. I found out I had postpartum depression. The problem was that I didn't know how to tell him. I was scared to tell him. Men didn't really understand what that meant and thought women could just snap out of it. Neither of us liked confrontation, so I just kept telling him no when he'd try to have sex with me."

"Oh no, Keisha."

"Yeah. When I found out he was cheating the first time, I was devastated but I knew it was my fault for not talking to him. At that point, I felt it was too late. He'd already done the inevitable. A couple of weeks after that woman showed up at our house, telling me she was pregnant, I fell victim to the smooth talk of another man. I cheated on Kenny."

Tiffany's mouth fell open, then she frowned slightly. "Before you continue, does Kenny know this and everything else you about to say to me?"

"Yes."

She nodded, then exhaled, dragging her face down her hand. "Okay. Sorry for interrupting you."

"I didn't just cheat. We practically had a relationship. It lasted for years. What I just found out before moving back was that Kenny knew about it the entire time but didn't say anything."

Her nostrils had flared out, so I brought my gaze to my fingers because I knew she was about to unleash on me. Not one to disappoint, she said, "You bitch. So, you drug my brother's name through the mud and treated him like shit for years when you were doing the same fucking thing? It takes a cold bitch to pull off some shit like that. Why are you here now? Are you giving him hope that y'all will be married again or some shit? Why the fuck are you here?"

She was on her feet, pacing back and forth in front of me. I knew if my answer wasn't what she wanted to hear, she would pop me in the mouth. "When he told me he knew, I crumbled before him. It was impossible to keep the charade going after that. I never stopped loving Kenny. I was angry, hurt, and most of all embarrassed. I didn't ask him to take me back. He moved me back here so the kids could be close to him and allowed me to stay here too. I believe what changed his attitude towards me was when we found out we'd been targeted. Someone close to him had set us up, knowing we were both too vulnerable to resist advances from the opposite sex. After Kenny had told him of our marital difficulties, he underhandedly sent Shardae to 'empt Kenny. It worked. Then he came after me, knowing I would be 'nerable about Kenny cheating. That worked, too."

'Who in the fuck would want to setup Kenny? How did y'all find 't out? Kenny gets along with everybody."

٭ I told Kenny that he somehow swindled me out of money

that I'd taken from him, the shit hit the fan. He also knew that Kenny had cheated on me. Kenny knew it was a setup, then."

"Who is he? Who did you cheat with for years?"

She was standing directly in front of me and I braced myself before saying, "Reggie."

Just as I thought she might, Tiffany slapped the shit out of me. Then turned her head and screamed. "My fucking ex? So, after I broke up with him, you fucked him? You sick bitch!"

"Tiffany, I was sleeping with him a year or so before y'all hooked up. I didn't sleep with him while he was with you."

"I see why Kenny didn't tell me. You a backstabbing hoe."

She grabbed her purse and walked out, slamming the door behind her. I sat on the sofa and cried my eyes out. My face was stinging, so I got up and went to the kitchen to get some ice. I deserved every bit of what she gave me and more. I walked up the stairs and went to Kendrick's room. Knowing how much he suffered, that slap from Tiff was nothing in comparison to that. Staring at his favorite fire truck, I smiled as I had memories of him making the siren noise as he pushed it. Even with the pain and heartache I was feeling, there were no more secrets. I felt free of guilt now.

Grabbing Kendrick's fire truck, I rolled it back and forth and made a soft siren noise as the tears rolled down my cheeks. My sweet baby. As I sat there crying, I noticed Kenny standing in the doorway. I quickly wiped my face and stood to leave the room. "I'm... I'm sorry. I was just trying to remember the happy times."

"Why are you apologizing? There's nothing to apologize for," he said with a slight frown.

After glancing down at the ice in my hand, he grabbed my chin and tilted my head to the side. "What happened to your face, Keisha?"

"I uh... I talked to Tiffany. I told her everything."

He tried to walk away, but I grabbed him by the shirt. "Kenny, I didn't want you to be bothered with telling her. You have enough pressure on you."

"She shouldn't have put her hands on you."

"I deserved it. Please. Just let it be. Okay?"

He looked over my head, trying to avoid my eyes. "Kenny... it's okay. I feel free now. There are no more secrets. Everything's out in the open. No more hiding."

He pulled me in his arms and held me close, then kissed my forehead. Tiffany had my damn ear ringing and I had a headache from hell. She hit me hard as fuck. "Come downstairs and take some Tylenol. If I know Tiff like I know I do, she rang that bell on yo' ass."

I was glad he could joke about the shit. I gave him the side-eye and he chuckled, then led me downstairs. I sat on the couch as he got me a bottle of water. "Have you heard from the detective yet?"

"Yeah. They will be here later today. Price wanted to come by and see you. I told him to come on by."

"Okay. Could you take those pork chops out the oven, baby?"

He smiled and said, "Yeah."

They smelled amazing and I was hungry as hell. He raised the lid on the roaster pan and sniffed. "Damn, this looks so good. You want me to fix you something?"

"Please? I'm starving. I don't know what I was expecting with Tiff, but I really didn't expect her to hit me. Well, in the back of my mind, I knew it was possible, but I still wanted to think that she wouldn't. I figured I'd be called a bitch, hoe, or whatever, but I didn't expect this."

Kenny smirked as I rolled my eyes. "I'm just glad she only hit you once. I know you wouldn't have hit her back because she's pregnant, but baby girl got a temper. So, if anything, I'm surprised she only hit you once."

I rolled my eyes as he brought my plate of baked pork chops, greens, carrots, and macaroni and cheese to the couch and sat it on the coffee table in front of me. "Thank you, baby. Fix Price a plate," I said as the doorbell rang.

That was probably him at the door. Kenny went to it and let Price in, but I was surprised to see Tiffany walk in, too. I almost stopped fucking breathing. I couldn't take another lick like that without striking back. I stood from my seat and hugged Price. "Hey, Keisha! It's so good to see you! Kendall is gonna be hurt she didn't get to see you."

Kendall was his wife. She was a sweetheart. "It's good to see you, too," I said as I noticed Tiffany talking quietly to Kenny in the kitchen. "How's Cassie?"

"Oh, baby girl is fine. She's almost twelve now. The twins are two."

"Twins? Wow! Girls or boys?"

"A boy and a girl."

"That's amazing. I'm so happy for you."

"Thanks."

"Price, come eat," Kenny said as he sat his plate on the table.

"Hell, yeah. Thanks, Keisha."

"You're welcome."

When Price walked away, Tiffany came sat next to me. For a while, she didn't say anything. I knew she was having a hard time with this, but she must've felt bad for hitting me. Otherwise, she wouldn't be back so soon. I grabbed my plate from the coffee table and turned to her slowly and said, "You want some? Kenny can fix you a plate."

I had to turn my head slowly, because my ear was still ringing. Yeah, she fucked me up with one blow. She shook her head. She turned to me and gently rubbed her hand down my cheek where the bruise was. "I'm sorry, Keisha," she whispered.

Tears fell down her cheeks and I knew it was the pregnancy making her emotional. Tiff was never a crier. Price and Kenny laughed loudly, so I glanced over at them, then looked back at her. "You didn't have to tell me. Although I would have charged Kenny up about it at a later date, you could have waited until he'd talked to me. Reggie don't mean shit to me. So, I don't know why I got so angry."

"I wasn't loyal. After y'all dated, I shouldn't have gone back to his bed. I shouldn't have drug Kenny's name through the cow shit, knowing all the mess I was engaged in. I deserved that hit and more. However, I'm not gon' let you get away with hitting me again."

Tiffany giggled, then said, "Shut yo' ratchet ass up."

I sat my food on the coffee table and hugged her. When I let her go and had picked up my food again, she pinched off a piece of my pork chop. After putting it in her mouth, her eyes rolled back as she chewed. "Oh my God, I missed your cooking."

I chuckled, then said, "Kenny, can you fix Tiff a plate?"

"Tell her to bring her greedy ass to her house and eat."

Tiffany sprang up from the couch to go give Kenny hell as I slowly shook my head. I was glad he was feeling good right now, but I knew it would be a different story when that detective got here.

17

K enny

"WHEN WE GOT THERE, SHE WAS STILL THERE WITH HIS BODY. She wasn't trying to run. I think she was starting to regret what she'd done, but it was too late. She had a note written. I think she had every intent to kill herself afterwards, but we showed up too soon."

My eyebrows had gone up. The detective had gotten here to let us know that Tasha had been arraigned this morning and they'd remanded her until her trial. Lucky her. I was prepared to get at her if they'd set bail. If I had to bail her out my damn self, I would have. I hesitantly took the letter from the detective as Keisha wrapped her arms around mine. I almost didn't want to read it, but I knew it would plague me if I didn't. When I opened it, I could see the water stains on it. I didn't feel sorry, that only infuriated me.

If I can't be happy, no one will. I only wanted this baby because I thought Kenny and I would have a future together. If not that, then he would at least have to take care of me until Kendrick was eighteen. What I didn't expect was for him to fight me for custody. Stingy muthafucka. So, here I was having to take care of a baby for free at first. Then he had the nerve to look just like Kenny's ass. I should've never had him. I never wanted children anyway, but I looked at it as an opportunity to lock down somebody that had something in life. I should have known he wouldn't want my ghetto ass. I was too ratchet to be his, but I was good enough to fuck. Well, since he wants to be dad of the fucking decade, I'm gon' show him better than I can tell him. I hold the fucking power to his happiness and his anguish. Fuck nigga. Now deal with life without your son.

I could feel my body trembling as I read that bullshit. She was a hateful-ass bitch. "I hope y'all bury her ass under the jail for this," I said as the tears fell from my eyes. "This is premeditated murder and torture of a child. An innocent child that trusted his mommy to take care of him. Stupid bitch!"

I stood from the couch and paced back and forth as the detective watched me. "I'm sorry, Mr. Henderson. I know this is hard, but the D.A. is going to prosecute her to the full extent of the law. This was a heinous crime and she's going to do a lot of time for this."

"How much time we talking?"

"Probably as much as twenty-five years or even life."

I rolled my eyes and said, "She need the fucking death penalty. My son suffered. He was an innocent baby. How could she do that shit?"

I sat back next to Keisha, trying to calm myself down as she rubbed my back. I could feel the tremble in her hands. This shit had ripped the scab that was trying to form over my wounds and poured alcohol in it. I was itching to get to Tasha. "When is her trial date set for?"

"In a month. May eighteenth."

Keisha leaned against me as I nodded. It had been a long fucking day. I'd been anticipating this shit since nine this morning, for almost eight hours. The detective stood from his seat, so I stood too as he said, "Again, I'm so sorry for your loss. If you guys need anything, please call us. We'll be in touch before the trial to give you more details about what to expect."

I nodded once again and escorted him to the door. When he left, I went back to the couch. Keisha held my hand in hers and we sat there quietly. She'd taken a nap after Price and Tiffany left and Tiffany had gotten the kids from school for us. I didn't want them here while the detective was here. The gravesite service was tomorrow, and I wasn't ready to bid farewell to my son. Keisha rubbed my hand and said, "Let me get a comb so I can braid your hair. I have a fresh style in mind."

"Maybe tomorrow night, baby. Kendrick loved when my hair was loose. I'd sing the little song from the *Lion King* to him. You know the one... In the Jungle, the mighty jungle, a lion sleeps tonight," I sang, then gave her a small smile.

She smiled back. "I miss your singing. Well, let me braid it back in a few big braids so it can look crimped and a little more straightened."

"Okay."

She stood from her seat on the couch as I thought about my lil man. At least he wasn't suffering now. I didn't know what quality of life he would have had if he would've made it through that. Letting the memories flow through my mind of his face when I would sing to him and how he would play in my hair when I sat him on my shoulders made me smile. While he was cranky a lot of our time together, I wouldn't trade it for the world. Once he'd gotten used to me and I had gotten my emotions in check, we were inseparable.

As I sat there, thinking about the past year with him in my life, I couldn't help but smile. Kendrick had kept me sane when I was missing my other babies. Maybe the Lord had put him here for that purpose. There was no telling what type of depression I would have sank into if I didn't have him to take care of. Maybe he was God's little angel that wasn't meant to live here on Earth. I wish his departure didn't have to be so painful, though.

When Keisha came back with a comb and some oil, I smiled at her and slid to the floor. She sat on the couch behind me and began playing in my hair. That was something she always loved to do. She loved my hair and that was the main reason I never cut it. I loved for her to play in it. Then when she left, God gave me Kendrick to prepare me for her return. As she greased my scalp, I lifted her foot and kissed the top of it. I was grateful she was here, because if I would have had to go through this alone, there was no telling how it would have all turned out.

I closed my eyes and let a deep moan leave me as she massaged my scalp. That always felt so good. "What time is Tiffany bringing the kids home?"

"I told her that I would go get them. It's not like they're going to school tomorrow."

"Right."

She began parting my mane and braiding it, not wasting anymore time. Within twenty minutes she was done. She'd braided it into five braids for me. "Thank you, baby."

I stood from my seat on the floor and pulled her to a standing position as well. Thankfully, she was milk chocolate complexioned. That bruise wasn't as noticeable. I gently rubbed my fingers down her face. "You're welcome, Kenny."

I grabbed her hand as she grabbed the comb and oil and led her upstairs. She went to the bathroom and put it up, then washed her hands as I continued to our bedroom. Although she didn't always sleep with me in there, she had been since Kendrick had died. When Keisha joined me in the room, I pulled her to me and kissed her deeply. Resting my forehead against hers, I said, "I don't know how I would have gotten through this without you. I love you."

"I love you so much, Kenny. I don't know how you were able to forgive me, but I'm so grateful you did."

"I'm done thinking about that, but I need you to forgive yourself. Okay?"

"Okay," she said softly as I slid the straps of her tank top off her shoulders.

She moaned as the top slid off her hard nipples. I went to it, flicking the piercing she had there with my tongue. She held onto my head as I squeezed her thighs. Keisha was so damn sexy, it was hard keeping my hands to myself. Now that I'd ended my celibacy, I couldn't get enough of her. Ever since the night of Kendrick's death, I'd found myself buried inside of her every chance I got. I slid her pants off as I kissed her skin, blazing a trail to where I wanted my tongue to get its greatest workout.

She moaned in satisfaction as I kissed her mound, then pushed her backwards to the bed. When she fell to it, I pulled her pants and underwear off completely and stared at her pussy as it leaked for me. I licked my lips, then went in, taking her essence on my tongue and savoring it for just in case I ever lost it again. I had no intentions of ever letting her go again, though. I tongue kissed it with all the love and passion I could muster, giving her my soul to do with as she pleased. I worshipped her heat for the wonder of the world it was. Before I could suck her clit, she was cumming on my lips, filling my taste buds with her premium nectar. "Kenny, fuck! Oh my God!"

Her legs trembled with the intensity of an earthquake and before she could stop cumming, I yanked my pants and underwear down and filled her with the beef she loved so much. "Damn, Keisha, I love you."

"I... love you... too, Kenny! Shit!"

I stroked her with a new passion and deeper desire than ever before, especially when I noticed she was wearing her ring. Leaning forward, I grabbed her hand and looked at it as she wrapped her legs around my waist. "You wanna be my wife again, Keisha?"

"That goes without saying, Kendrall. I will always be yours, anyway."

"Kendrall, huh?"

"Uh huh. Kendrall Dominic Henderson."

"Girl, you almost made me bust. Say my name like that again."

"Kendrall Dominic Henderson. Fuck me, please!"

No more words were spoken after that. Only grunts from me, moans from the both of us, and screams from her. Seeing her titties bouncing when she rode me and that ass jiggling when I hit it from the back was enough to pull the beast out a nigga. I rough rode her ass until I was grunting out my release right into her depths. Releasing her legs, I laid on top of her, and kissed her neck. "Keisha?"

"Yes, baby?"

"That felt like the first time we had sex. You remember it?"

"How could I forget it? I was visiting Nome for the first time and you'd introduced everyone to me. This felt a lot like the sex after you proposed, in my opinion."

"Hmm. Well, we've never had bad sex. Sometimes it was just more passion filled."

"Right."

"Well, you relax, and I'll go get the kids. We have a long day tomorrow."

"Yeah," she said as the tear fell from her eye.

I swallowed hard and wiped her tear away, not looking forward to tomorrow my damn self.

❧

As the preacher prayed, I just wanted this moment to be over. Seeing his little casket in front of me was devastating to my emotions. I'd cried more today than I had in the past few days combined. All my family, including Legend, Red, and Zay, were here to support me as well as Price and Shylou. Keisha's friend, Cass, had even come from San Antonio. Lots of people from our small community had driven to Claybar's Cemetery in China for support as well. I stared at the casket, allowing the tears to flow. I'd had it customized. Paw Patrol characters were all over the outside of it. His spirit had to be screaming in excitement at those characters surrounding his body.

When the preacher finally said amen, I stood from my seat with

Keisha and my kids and walked to the casket. Laying my hand on it, I closed my eyes as my hair blew in the breeze. After taking a deep breath, I began singing our Lion King song. As I sang, Karima grabbed my hand and sang with me. When I got to the A-weema-weh's it seemed the whole family was singing with me. It was like in that moment, my heart was freed from the heaviness. When we were done, I wiped my face and leaned over and kissed his casket. "Rest, well son."

The kids and Keisha all did the same. I stood there for a moment, just staring and trying to pull myself away. No one pressured or rushed me. They just stood there in silent support. After a few minutes, I took a deep breath and turned to walk away, leaving my son forever.

My parents, along with my sisters, prepared a repast at the main barn on the highway. When we got there, I took a deep breath and exhaled slowly. While the services were over, I knew I still had a long way to go to recover. Grief would live in my heart for a while, but I would do my best to continue on with life, holding on to Kendrick's memory.

When we got out of the car, I shook hands and hugged numerous people before getting to the barn. I noticed the balloons and stuffed animals everywhere and smiled. Kendrick would have gone crazy. His first birthday party was the same way. It was here at the main barn and he was so excited to see the decorations. When we got inside, Storm was at the door waiting for us. He hugged me tightly and led us to our seats. When I saw him crying at the funeral, I knew that my baby's death was hard for everyone in attendance to accept.

After sitting, I looked around and noticed the pictures of him strategically placed around the barn and the Lion King Soundtrack was playing softly. My family had made this repast feel like a birthday party and I appreciated them for that. "Dad, Kendrick would have been screaming and laughing. This looks like his birthday party," KJ said with a smile on his face.

"Yep. I wouldn't have been able to do a thing with him."

I chuckled at memories of his birthday party. Shylou came and sat next to me as my Mama sat plates of spaghetti, salad, and cornbread in front of me and Keisha. "Man, this may not be the appropriate time, but you see that thick goddess heading this way?"

I gave him a one-cheeked smile. "Uh huh."

"Who is that?"

"Keisha's friend, Cass."

"Oh yeah? I'ma need you to hook that up. I don't wanna just approach her at this repast, but I need a way in."

"She's staying at our house until Thursday."

"Well, you don't say. I guess I'm gon' be there later today and tomorrow then."

"You barely come to my house, but since you think you done found something exciting to get into, you know where I live."

"I see you at the convenience store all the time. What I need to go to your house for? Ain't shit be going on over there."

"Oh there's plenty going on, now."

Shylou turned his lip up as I laughed. He patted my back and said, "Whatever. Just mention a nigga. That's all I ask."

He glanced over at Cass and she and Keisha were looking our way. "How you doing, Keisha?" Shylou said, then gave Cass a smile.

I rolled my eyes as he winked, and Cass turned red. "She feeling a nigga, too. I don't even need yo' ass, Kendrall."

I pushed him, causing him to laugh, then continued eating my spaghetti, Kendrick's favorite meal. He went to the table with Price and his family, but not before telling me to hook that up. When Keisha got up to go to the restroom, Cass took her seat and hugged my neck. She kissed my cheek and said, "I'm so glad you and Keisha worked this shit out. I told her that despite everything, you were a good man to and for her. I'm not gon' lie, when she first showed me a picture of you years ago, I was smitten. And don't think I'm coming on to you, because I would never, but I do wanna know more about your boy. What's his name?"

I rolled my eyes once again. "Shylou. Why don't you go talk to him? Y'all are both asking about each other. I'm sure he's gonna make his way to the house."

She frowned slightly. "Shylou is his real name?"

"Yep."

"That's different, but it fits his sex appeal."

"A'ight. I don't like where this conversation is going."

"Aww whatever, Kenny. Your sex appeal is taken, so don't knock somebody else's."

"I'm not knocking it. I just don't wanna hear about it," I said as Keisha made her way back to the table with a slight frown on her face.

"Umm, Cass, get away from my man."

Cass rolled her eyes as I laughed. "Shit, whatever. I'm tryna get the 4-1-1 on Shylou sexy ass."

I tuned out the rest of their conversation and finished my spaghetti, so I could mingle a bit. Storm and Jasper were talking to Legend, Red, and Zay as Price and Shylou made their way to them as well. I looked around for WJ just to see if he'd made it and I found him over to the side talking to Dad and Marcus. I was willing to bet that was why Storm had a frown on his face. Had we been here for anything else, he would have approached him by now. Before I could get up to throw my plate in the trash, my mama sat next to me. "How you doing, baby?"

"I'm doing okay. This is beautiful what y'all did. I appreciate it."

She smiled as the tear fell down her cheek. She played in my hair a bit and said, "Yeah. I'm gonna miss my little munchkin."

Before Keisha had come back, Kendrick spent a lot of time with my mama while I was handling business. He called her Gamma, since he couldn't say grandma. I put my arm around her shoulders and kissed her head. "I know. We're all gonna miss him."

She stood from her seat and took my plate. I could tell she was trying to keep moving so she wouldn't have time to think about him and cry. "Mama?"

"Yes, baby?"

151

I stood from my seat and pulled her back in my arms. "It's okay."

She sat the plate on the table and wrapped her arms around my waist and cried her eyes out. My brothers, including WJ, all surrounded us, offering their love and showing their concern for the woman that meant everything to us. Once she finally calmed down, she lifted her head from my chest. "I'm sorry Kenny. You're trying to bear enough of your own."

"Mama, my hands and heart are never too full for you. Okay?"

She nodded, then kissed my cheek. When she grabbed my plate and walked away, Storm put his arm around her and walked with her to the serving area where people had begun to help themselves. There was plenty left over, and I surely didn't want to have to bring it all home. I walked over to where the music was playing and put on some Zydeco. I'd had enough of the Lion King for one day. Several turned their heads like they wanted to dance, and I chuckled. "Y'all have a good time!" I yelled, then went talked to my boys.

While I was sure they would all be at the house later with their families, I needed to get out of the frame of mind I was sinking to. Keisha was having a great time catching up with Cass, so I figured I would try to have a great time as well, despite the circumstances.

❧ 18 ❧

K eisha

"You know you missed the fuck outta my ass! So, quit playing."

I laughed as I got dressed. Cass was right. I missed her so damn much, even though we talked or texted almost every day. "You right. I missed you so much."

"So, how have things been going since the baby died? You okay?"

"No. I loved him like he was mine, surprisingly. I always thought that I wouldn't be able to raise him because of the circumstances, but I was so wrong. He was the sweetest little boy, Cass, and I don't know how I'm going to be strong for Kenny when I can't seem to be strong for myself. When I went to the bathroom at the repast, it was so I could cry. I was home with him a lot this past month and a half. He'd started calling me Ma-Ma. How do I get over that?"

Cass rushed over to me and held me close as I cried. Yesterday had been so hard. She and I didn't really get a chance to talk because everyone had stayed late into the night, making sure we were okay. Today, Kenny had gone to the convenience store and Cass and I were supposed to be going to lunch. The kids had gone back to school today, so it would be just me and her. When they got out of school, Kenny was supposed to be taking KJ to practice cutting. KJ was getting better and better at it and would probably be entering a rodeo to compete soon.

When Cass let me go, she said, "I hate this happened. That baby didn't deserve that. When is that bitch's trial?"

"Less than a month from now. If I could, I'd kill her. That kick in the mouth she got two years ago ain't got shit on what I want to do to her now."

"I feel you. If I could, I'd bail her ass out of jail just to fuck her up."

"Kenny said the same thing."

"I see things have been great between the two of you. I'm so happy for you. I really thought you had lost your damn mind. You know I was team Kenny almost the whole time."

I rolled my eyes and said, "Yeah, yeah. But we are really good. It feels like it did when were engaged. Everything seems so fresh. I love it."

"Well, I gave Shylou my phone number. He said he was gonna hit me up tonight. Can you believe that? I'm gon' have a man before I leave from here. Just watch. Cass and Shylou. That sound good as hell."

I slid on my wedding ring, then pulled my dreads loose as Cass gave me a cynical smile, similar to the way Storm did when he had something up his sleeve. "What?"

"You put on your ring."

"It's my ring and we're doing everything married people do. Even fucking without condoms."

Her eyebrows shot up. "Bitch! You gon' mess around and get pregnant. Are you on birth control?"

"Nope. I told Kenny that I wasn't, but it seems he doesn't care. I'm thinking it's because of what happened to Kendrick. We had sex for the first time, the same night he died. I think he wants a baby. But I'll have to talk to him. Having another baby isn't going to make dealing with Kendrick's death any easier."

She shook her head as her phone chimed. It must have been Shylou because she was all smiles. She hadn't had a boyfriend in years, so I was hoping that they hit it off. After getting my shoes on, I sent Kenny a text to let him know we were about to leave and that I would call him when we were heading back. Once I was done getting myself together, we headed to Beaumont to go to Chuck's Sandwich Shop. I had to introduce Cass to their chicken potatoes. The first time I tasted it, I fell in love and I knew she would do the same. It was a huge spud filled with fried chicken bites, cheese, and a cream gravy. I didn't even like cream gravy like that, but on that spud, it was amazing.

Once we had gotten there and had ordered our food, I got a text message from Kenny. *Where did y'all go for lunch? Me and Shylou gonna come meet y'all.*

We're at Chuck's, baby. We just got here.

Cass wasn't gon' know what to do with herself when Shylou walked through that door. After getting our drinks, we sat close to the window in front and put our order number to the edge of the table. Before we could start a conversation, the door chimed. Out of natural habit, I looked to see who came in and nearly swallowed my tongue. It was Reggie. I hurriedly turned my head as Cass watched me with a frown on her face. "What's wrong wit'chu?"

I couldn't respond to her because he'd noticed me and headed straight to our table. *Shit. Hurry up, Kenny.* He smiled and said, "Hello, Keisha. How are you?"

I looked up at him and refused to back down. "Hey. I'm good. How's your arm?"

He smirked, then said, "It's cool. Nothing that won't heal eventually." He looked over to Cass and licked his lips as she and I frowned. "Hello. I'm Reginald, but everyone calls me Reggie."

He extended his hand as Cass's eyes widened slightly. "Hello. I'm Cass, Keisha's *best* friend."

She put emphasis on the word 'best' to probably let him know that she knew all about him. She never shook his hand, so he awkwardly took it back. He nodded, then said, "You ladies have a good lunch."

When he walked away and got in line, I exhaled. "Girl! That muthafucka got nerve!" Cass whispered harshly. "Didn't the Hendersons..."

"Yes. Shhh," I said, shushing her.

You never knew who was eavesdropping on our conversation. Before Reggie could sit down, Kenny and Shylou had entered and I was thanking God for his grace and mercy. Reggie looked like he wanted to come sit with us. Kenny frowned when he saw him, but he didn't say anything. He and Shylou went to order their food as the waiter brought ours. "Enjoy, ladies."

"Thank you."

"Keisha, this shit look so good. Almost better than Shylou's ass over there. Damn, he so fine."

She winked at him and he licked his lips and winked back. I rolled my eyes slightly and indulged in my potato. "Kenny look hot as shit. He probably mad that nigga here."

"You think?"

I slid my hand down my face and looked over at Kenny and Shylou walking towards us. When they sat with their drinks, Shylou grabbed Cass's hand and kissed it. "How you doing, beautiful?"

She was blushing and shit like that nigga was LaKeith Stanfield or somebody. Kenny sat next to me and kissed my cheek. "Hey, baby. He tried to talk to you?"

"He did. He came over, spoke and introduced himself to Cass and asked how we were doing."

"He trying me. We're in a public place, but I'm gon' catch his ass eventually."

"He's already gotten fucked up once. I don't know why he insists on even speaking to us. We're Hendersons. I'll flip all this shit over in here."

Kenny smirked at me as I fed him some of my potato. The way he looked at me when he pulled that shit off the fork had me ready to get out of here. Fuck that potato. After he swallowed his food, he kissed me, allowing it to linger a bit. "Umm, we are in a public place. Maybe y'all should get a room and leave the table to more civilized adults like me and Shylou."

Shylou said something in her ear and she giggled. It was like they'd been knowing one another forever. "Tell 'em, Cass," he mumbled.

"I'm going to extend my stay if that's okay with you guys. Instead of leaving tomorrow, I'd like to stay through the weekend."

I smiled brightly, then frowned when I realized why she was staying. "So, you using us like a hotel."

"Pretty much, baby," Kenny chimed in.

"Aww, come on, Keish. Don't be like that."

I rolled my eyes, then smiled at her. "Fine. You better be glad Kenny likes you."

"My brother-in-law more than likes me. He loves my ass, 'cause I give it to y'all straight."

When the waiter brought Kenny and Shylou's food, I could see Reggie watching us and I believed Kenny saw him, too. Kenny put his fork in the potato and said, "Shit. It's too hot, so I might as well kill some time."

I tried to hold his arm to keep him from getting up, but he gave me a look like he gave me in San Antonio when he'd come to visit. I quickly released him and watched him walk over to Reggie's table. He sat in front of him, so I decided to walk over, too, and sit next to Kenny. I couldn't have my man going to jail over no bullshit-ass nigga like Reggie. Weak muthafucka. When I sat next to Kenny, he pulled me in his arms. "Since you seem to want conversation, I'm about to give it to you. You a grimy, weak-ass muthafucka. I don't mind saying what I have to say, but since you already knew what you did, I didn't think I had to. Obviously, you done caught amnesia. You owe me a hundred grand, and if you keep fucking with me, I'm gon' get it out'cho ass. Secondly, this is my wife. You might have succeeded last time, but this time, I'll cut yo' fucking nuts off if you try it again. I hope you got me."

Reggie just stared at Kenny, like he was in shock that Kenny even walked over. "The only reason I didn't press charges on y'all was because of the situation with your *ex*-wife. I need my job and that goes against the ethics clause in my contract. I didn't force her to give me a thing. She gave it to me, because she fell in love with me. But let me clarify something. I always told her I would pay her back. I followed her here to pay her back. There's one hundred grand in my car. That's with interest, because she gave me a total of ninety-four thousand, five hundred dollars. Anything else, Kendrall?"

"Yeah. If I didn't want to leave my babies behind, I would have fucking killed you. You grimy and I saw you do it to somebody else, but I never thought you would have turned on me. But now I know. A snake don't care who he bites. My wife," he said, holding up my hand, "Was off-limits."

"And let me clarify something right quick. Reggie, I did have feelings for you, but I never fell in love with you. Kenny Henderson is the only man I love. So, don't fool yourself. You will never be the man that he is, no matter how hard your jealous ass tries. That's what this all boils down to. You're jealous of the man he is and the financial power he has. Get over it and live your damn life."

Although we hadn't gotten remarried, I knew that we would, and furthermore, I was his wife when Reggie approached me. Before Reggie could respond, the woman I remembered as Shardae, walked in the café and sat next to him. She was pregnant. I glanced over at Kenny to see he had turned red as hell. "Kenny, you remember Shardae, right? This is my wife."

Kenny grabbed my hand and stood, so I did the same. "Let's go, before I do something I'll regret."

"Kenny, look. It's over and done with. I won't speak to you, your wife, or your kids. Once I give you your money, can we just move on?"

Kenny didn't justify him with an answer. Instead, we went back to our table and I asked the waiter for a box. My appetite was ruined. While I was glad Kenny was able to restrain himself from knocking Reggie out, he'd made me nervous with the threats he delivered. I was hoping Reggie's punk ass wasn't recording him. Kenny brought a forkful of potato and chicken to his mouth as I watched him. He grabbed my hand as he chewed, and said, "Don't worry. I'm cool. Once he gives me my money, this is over, unless he does something else. In that case, I'll have to make good on my threats. But while he tryna act hard in this café, I promise you, he heard me. He only gon' flex when he has an audience."

Shylou was nodding, agreeing with Kenny. I hoped he was right, because I was ready for all that shit to just be over.

❧

"Mommy, where did Daddy and KJ go?"

"KJ is practicing so he can sign up to compete in a rodeo."

"Is he gonna be on a horse?"

"Yes, baby girl."

It had been a day for the books. Chasity and I had to sit down and go over Kenny's financials to be sure there were no discrepancies. I remembered that she did that every three months for him. But now that he'd gotten that loan to build the truck stop, it was imperative that he kept things tight. He was also talking about starting an ambulance service. So, he really had to be on his shit. Price had completed all the dirt work already and once he did, he and his wife, Kendall, and their kids came to visit. We'd had a great time and it seemed KJ

159

and Cassie were getting along as well. She could keep up with him on that game.

It had been two weeks since we'd seen Reggie and he had given Kenny his money. I couldn't believe that he had married the chick that had helped him set us up. That alone proved it was a game to them. I was beyond surprised when he gave Kenny his money back, though. "Sit up, baby. I'm almost finished."

I was braiding Karima's hair, because she wanted it to look like Kenny's. These kids loved their daddy. Whatever he did, they wanted to do. KJ's hair was almost long enough to where I would be able to braid it as well. "Mommy, why can't I ride the horse?"

"You can. Let your dad know, and I'm sure he'll get Aunt Tiffany to help you if you want to compete in something like your brother."

"Did you ride horses?"

"Not until I met your dad. He taught me how to ride."

She was quiet for a moment and I was glad the questions had ceased. She'd been talking since I started on her hair and it had been an hour. When her head bobbed, I realized she'd stopped talking because she'd fallen asleep. I chuckled, then leaned her head against my leg, so I could get done with the last couple of braids. Being that it was Friday evening, I just let her sleep. We didn't have much to do tomorrow, either.

As I finished her last braid, the doorbell rang. Wiping my hands on the towel next to me, I laid Karima on the pillow next to her and went to see who it was. I was pretty sure it was family. No one just dropped by unless it was one of Kenny's brothers or Tiffany. Jenahra and Chrissy usually called first if they were going to come by. The two of them had become true introverts. We weren't nearly as close as we were before I left, but I knew that had a lot to do with me. Without looking to see who it was, I opened the door to see WJ standing there. "Hey, Keisha. Is Kenny home? I was passing by and figured I'd stop so he and I could talk."

"No, he's not here. He's helping KJ get practice with cutting."

He smiled and said, "I remember when Kenny was getting into that. I was proud of my little brother."

He ran his hand over his face and took a deep breath. "Listen. I'm sorry for everything. The disrespect was uncalled for. Truth was, I was jealous. Sharon is a good woman, don't get me wrong, but you were damn near superwoman. When Kenny would brag about all the shit you used to do, instead of me being happy for him, I envied him. His marriage seemed so perfect, unlike mine. Sharon and I argued a lot. But I know the reason it seemed perfect. At the time, you were both doing what it took to make your marriage work. When it came to my marriage, I was lazy and didn't wanna put the work in."

After rolling his eyes and shaking his head, he continued. "I thought the situation between us was over and done with, but when it came up again, I realized that I hadn't handled it right. Instead of pushing it under the rug and pretending nothing happened, I should've come to you, like I am now, to apologize. And then, the way I talked to you when you left Kenny... I'm so sorry, Keisha."

"Thank you for that, WJ. I really appreciate that. All is forgiven."

He held his hand out for a handshake, but I gave him a hug. When I released him, he looked like he wanted to cry. "I don't know how I allowed myself to fuck things up with my family."

I glanced back at Karima to see she was still asleep, then walked outside, leaving the door open. She would be able to see us through the storm door Kenny had installed. I sat on the porch and WJ sat as well. "When you aren't happy, you tend to want to make the people around you miserable. Are you happy, WJ?"

"Honestly, I haven't been for a long time. When Sharon cheated on me, I never recovered. I tried to talk myself into believing that I'd forgiven her, but I never did. Whenever I look at her, I get visions of her bending over for someone else. Those thoughts are going to drive me crazy. I love Sharon and accept responsibility for the role I played in the situation, but it's like I can't let go. Seeing my siblings all happy in their marriages made me bitter as hell. It caused me to do things unimaginable. I love my family, but I'm afraid that things will never be the same. Especially with my baby brother."

Storm had a temper out this world and was petty as hell. He didn't forgive easily. WJ definitely had a better chance with Kenny than with Storm or even Jasper and Tiffany for that matter. As we sat quietly, Kenny drove in the driveway. I could see the frown on his face and I silently prayed that things would go well between them. He and KJ got out the truck and headed toward us. KJ kissed my cheek, spoke to WJ, and headed in the house while Kenny stood there staring at him. He walked over to me and said, "Hey, baby. Everything okay?"

"Yeah, babe. I'm gonna go inside and give y'all some time."

I stood from my seat and walked in the house. After waking Karima up so she could see her hair, I watched her dance in the mirror. "Can you do my hair like this for my birthday next weekend?"

"Of course, baby."

She did the floss in the mirror as I laughed, then went to KJ's room to bother him. I looked across the hallway at Kendrick's room. Neither of us had gathered the strength to go inside and try to pack away his things. It wouldn't happen today, either. Going closer, I rested my hand on the door, then leaned my forehead against it. "I miss you so much, baby boy," I whispered.

After a few moments, I backed away from the door and went to my bedroom to take a moment to myself and get ready to feed my family, hoping that things were going well with Kenny and WJ.

❦ 19 ❧

K enny

"So you telling me that you were jealous of us? Why? I'm your brother."

"I know. It was stupid. It's still stupid. Jealousy can be a powerful thing when you feed into it. I fed it daily with my negative thoughts."

I sat there, thinking about everything WJ had said. He was my brother and I knew at some point, I needed to forgive him. Forgiveness wasn't for him, but for me. We sat there quietly for a while, at least ten minutes, without even looking at each other, before I finally said, "I forgive you, WJ. But it's gon' be longer before I feel comfortable around you."

"I understand, brother. Thank you for the opportunity to make it right."

He stood to his feet, so I did the same. Watching my big brother decline emotionally over the past three or four years had been hard.

He and Sharon definitely needed counseling. It seemed there were some things going on between them that he didn't want to talk about. As I held my hand out to shake his hand, he pulled me into an embrace. "Kenny, you've always been there for me. I'm gonna do my best to prove to you that you can trust me to be there for you, too."

I nodded as he smiled at me, then walked off the porch. "Now to Jasper and Tiffany's houses."

"Good luck. When are you going to Storm's?"

"Tomorrow morning. I'm gonna need every ounce of energy I got to deal with him."

I chuckled, then watched him get in his truck and leave. Walking inside, I saw Keisha in the kitchen preparing dinner. I walked over to her to see she'd cooked pork ribs, butter beans, rice, and potato salad. I kissed her neck and said, "I better get back on my workout routine quick. All this good cooking gon' have me fat as hell."

She giggled, then screamed after I swat her ass. "Go take a shower! You smell like cow shit!"

I laughed loudly. "Cow manure?"

"Same thing! It's shit!"

I laughed again and carried my stank ass upstairs. As I walked by Karima's room, I could see she was on her tablet. She was so interested in what she was watching, she never saw me standing there. I quietly walked in to see she was watching a video of a girl barrel racing. "What is the almost birthday girl doing in here?" I asked loudly, scaring her half to death.

"Daddy! You scared me!" she said, then pouted.

"I'm sorry baby girl, but it was funny."

"Can you teach me how to do this?"

"Nope, but I know somebody who can. Your Aunt Tiffany won a few buckles doing that exact thing."

"Really? You think she would teach me?"

"I think she would love to teach you. Maybe you can call her after dinner."

"Okay."

She was so excited, she quickly turned around to continue watching the video. I slowly shook my head as I left her room. Before making it to my room, I stopped in front of Kendrick's room and opened the door. At some point, I needed to get his things out of there, but at the same time, I wanted it to stay that way forever. I wanted the memories of him to remain fresh, like they'd happened yesterday. However, I knew that it would be unhealthy to hang on to him that way. I smiled slightly, then went to my room.

⊗⊗⊗

"MAN, THAT SHIT UGLY."

"I don't know what possessed me to bring your ass with me. I know what Keisha likes."

"Kenny, you know I'll be the first to tell Storm how wrong he is, but that really is ugly as shit," Jasper said.

Storm laughed as I handed the ring back to the jeweler. I felt like we were kids again and I got stuck babysitting them. "I should've brought Tiffany."

"She would've told you how ugly that shit was, too. Hol' on. Let me send her a picture of it."

I walked away from the two of them, looking for something else. Although I had been shopping for Karima's birthday, I decided to make a stop to look for a ring for Keisha. I refused to let her keep wearing the first one. We were doing everything new. While I was sure this wedding wouldn't be as big as the first one, it would mean just as much, if not more. Our lives were finally at a calm state to where I could focus on just how amazing our relationship had become. Even the kids had noticed that Keisha had been sleeping with me every night since we'd made love... and since Kendrick had died.

As I found another ring I liked, Storm and Jasper laughed loudly. They walked over to me and Storm said, "Tiff say who in the fuck that ugly shit belong to?"

"Let me see that," I said, snatching the phone from his hand.

Sure enough, that was exactly what she'd said... word for word. I slid my hand down my face. They laughed again, as the jeweler looked to be getting impatient. "Well, what do y'all think about this one?" I asked, pointing out the one I was now looking at.

"That's better, but it still ain't the one."

"Maybe another jeweler can help you gentlemen."

Oh shit. Storm was finna come unglued on his ass. Jasper smirked and leaned against the jewelry counter. Storm took off the crossbody bag I'd given him. He pulled out a couple of stacks and said, "I guess we'll be spending this shit somewhere else then."

The jeweler's eyes widened but his pride wouldn't let him recant. "His loss, Kenny."

"Right. I was prepared to spend quite a bit of money in here. Oh well."

We walked out of the store as the man watched us, probably regretting every minute. "Storm yo' loud ass got us kicked out the store," Jasper said.

"Man, fuck that dude. It ain't like we were scaring off other customers. We were the only muthafuckas in there."

"Neither one of y'all have class. Had I been in there by myself I would have had a ring by now."

"Yeah. That uglass muthafucka. Keisha would have had to fake the funk with that shit!"

Jasper and Storm cracked up as we went to another store. When we got there, I looked at the both of them. "Don't make me break out the belt. Act like y'all got some sense in this damn store!" I said, mimicking our mama.

We all fell out laughing. That was her warning whenever she took all of us to the store. Most times WJ stayed with Dad when we were younger. Jenahra and Chrissy had to help her keep us together. Storm and Tiffany would be running through clothing racks like it wasn't nothing. "We get kicked out of this store and I'm gon' leave y'all in the truck next time."

We made our way in the store while Jasper and Storm shushed each other, and I rolled my eyes. When I walked to the counter, the perfect ring was staring me in the face. "Yo... this is it, y'all."

"Let me see this shit," Storm said. When he walked closer, he said, "Oh, damn. I think that *is* it. Jasper come see."

We all agreed that I'd found the ring, but to be safe, Storm sent Tiff a picture. While we waited for her response, we looked around, but didn't find anything remotely close to that one in elegance, style, or beauty. It was a beautiful chocolate diamond ring, surrounded by round diamonds, on a rose gold band. Keisha would absolutely love that ring. "Tiff sent the wide-eyed emojis, so I guess that means it's beautiful. It really is Kenny. That's the one," Jasper said.

I nodded, then took the bag from Storm and got the jeweler's attention. "You found the one already?"

"Yes sir. It was staring me in the face."

When I pointed to it, he smiled and said, "It's a beautiful ring."

I nodded as I smiled at the image of Keisha's face that came to mind. When she was excited about something, her eyebrows lifted and scrunched together as her lips parted. I knew that would be her reaction when she saw this ring. It set me back almost twenty grand but it was worth every penny.

Once we were in the truck, Storm asked, "So when are you gonna pop the question? At Karima's party?"

"No. I think I wanna take her somewhere nice. Somewhere in Houston and propose to her there. But I think I'm gonna wait until the weekend after Karima's party. I don't wanna steal baby girl's thunder. Oh, and I meant to tell y'all, she wants to barrel race."

"That's what's up! Tiff gon' start working with her?" Jasper asked.

"Yeah. That's one of her birthday gifts. She gon' worry the hell out of Tiff."

They both laughed, then Jasper pat my shoulder. "You know, bruh, I'm really proud of you. I don't know how you overcame all that bullshit you went through. Then that shit with Reggie's ass would

167

have had me under the jail, 'cause I would have shot his mutha-fucking ass," Storm said.

"Yo! Speaking of... did you ever get at Marcus?" I asked.

A slow smile came to his lips and I didn't know what the hell that meant, but I knew it wasn't good. Jasper was doing his best not to laugh. "Hell yeah. So, I went to the grass farm to check on things and when I was about to leave, he was driving up. Of course, when I saw his ass, I parked. I got out the truck and he tried to get back in his. I was like, naw, what's up? What'chu doin' out here? He was nervous as hell and that was all the ammunition I needed. I jacked his ass up and threw him against the truck, then pulled my gun on his ass. That nigga pissed on himself. I put that gun right under his chin and told him if I ever see him anywhere near any of our property, I was gon' shoot his ass and I would be shooting to kill. When I let him down, he got out of there so fast, he almost hit the ditch."

I shook my head slowly. Marcus had brought that on himself. He should have known we wouldn't have taken too kindly to him fucking anything up being that he was the one killing off our cattle some years back when we found out he was our brother. I should have known it was gon' be some crazy shit involved if Storm got ahold of him.

After getting some things for baby girl's party, we headed back to Nome. I enjoyed spending time with my brothers. It was always a good time dealing with their asses. Before we could get to Nome, though, Shylou was calling. I answered with my Bluetooth. "What's up, bruh?"

"Yo, man. Listen. Baby girl wanna come visit."

"What? Who?"

"Cass wanna come visit. She wanna come stay with me."

"Aww shit. I guess you betta get yo' ratchet-ass baby mama out of there, then."

"Man... that has yet to be determined. We waiting on the test results and should be getting them any day now."

"Shylou! Why you got her living wit'cho ass then?" Storm yelled out.

"Aww shit! Why you didn't tell me that nigga was in the car?"

We all laughed and Shylou laughed, too. "She got evicted from her apartment because she got laid off. Until I can find her something else that's cheaper and safe, she staying with me."

"But why you gotta find her something else?"

"I don't have to, Storm, but that's what people who have a heart and are in a financial position to do so, do. I couldn't live with myself to see her living in a shelter or on the street. Had she told me beforehand about her eviction, I would have paid a month just so she wouldn't be in this bitch with me."

"So what'chu gon' do?" Jasper asked.

"How the hell you got both them niggas with you today?"

"We went ring shopping for Keisha."

"Well, shut the fuck up. I'm happy for you, bruh."

"Quit stalling, Shylou. What'chu gon' do about Cass?" Storm said.

"Nosy-ass nigga," Shylou mumbled. "I'on know yet. If I put her off too long, she gon' know something up. And shit, I been wanting to dig in that since I first saw her. Shawty fine as hell."

"She a'ight," I said. "But she ain't gon' play wit'cho ass long, though. So, I suggest you quit worrying about cheaper and quit being nice and get Tangeray's ass out of there now."

"Tangeray? Her name Tangeray? Oh hell naw," Storm said while laughing.

"Nigga, shut up sometimes!" Shylou said, then exhaled loudly.

"Shylou, I'm telling you. Get that chick out of your house. Pay one month's rent and when you find out if the kid is yours or not, decide what'chu gon' do, then."

"I agree," Jasper said. "If it ain't yours, she got a month to decide what the hell she gon' do. If it is yours, then keep paying rent for the time being until she find a job. How far along is she?"

"Man, she like eighteen weeks. Ain't nobody gon' hire her that late in the game. You can clearly see she's pregnant. I think I'm gon' ship her back to her family in New Orleans if it ain't mine."

Storm and Jasper laughed. "That nigga say ship her, like he bought her from Amazon," Jasper said.

I rolled my eyes at the two nuts in the truck with me. They could make a joke out of anything. "Shylou, in the meantime, get her in an apartment. Does Cass know about her?"

"She knows that I could possibly have a baby on the way, so yeah. Me and Cass aren't a couple right now. We just kicking it, but since she wanna come spend time with a nigga, I gotta get shit in order. We been talking on the phone for two weeks now, and after spending time with her when she was there, I know I gotta have her. We just clicked... like, we a lot alike."

"Well, do what'chu gotta do. It should be a no brainer. You ain't hurting for money, Shylou. So, quit being tight."

"A'ight. I'll see y'all at the party."

"A'ight."

I ended the call and Storm said, "Y'all niggas be in the strangest predicaments. If y'all just handled shit like I do and quit being all soft and shit, your shit would already be in order when the right woman came along. I fucked around, but the minute Aspen came along, a nigga was ready. I ain't have to break no hearts or deal with no issues."

"Well, everybody can't be a rude, mean ass muthafucka like you, Storm," I said and chuckled.

He shrugged his shoulders. "It ain't shit to it but to do it."

The rest of the conversation was about our women and how they completed us. My brothers had found some good women and I was happy that they were treating them right. I'd never imagined that Storm's mean ass would ever get married, but the right woman had come along and humbled him, found his calm and soft side. The way he loved her proved that. As I thought about the ring I left at the store to get sized, I knew without a shadow of a doubt that Keisha was the one for me. Despite all the shit we allowed to happen, she was the only woman I loved, and I knew I was the only man she loved as well.

✿ 2 0 ✿

K eisha

"CASS! I WASN'T EXPECTING YOU TO COME!"

Cass had shown up for Karima's seventh birthday party unannounced. I knew that shit had to do with Shylou. She was fiending to be next to that man, especially since he hadn't given her a date that she could go spend time with him at his house in Houston. I wondered what the holdup was. He was definitely feeling her. While I didn't know about Shylou's personal life, I knew that he was a good friend to Kenny just like Cass was an amazing friend to me. She hugged me tightly, then discreetly looked around the barn. "He's not here yet, hoe."

She pushed me in the arm and said, "Where's the birthday girl?"

"When she saw that horse her daddy bought her, that was it. She's in back, begging Tiffany to show her some things."

"Well, let me go tell her happy birthday. I wasn't looking for Shylou, by the way."

"Lies," I said as she laughed, then went to the back.

Everything was going well. The entire family was here and WJ was even talking to Storm and Jasper. I supposed all was well with everyone again and I couldn't be more grateful. Having tension in the air for my baby's party would be a no go. As I saw Kenny on his phone, I got a little concerned. He had a frown on his face, and he looked like he wanted to either cry or fuck something up. I stood next to him as he turned red, then he said into the receiver, "Thank you. I appreciate that. We'll be there."

After he ended the call, he grabbed me by the hand and escorted me out of the barn to the field next to it. "What's going on, baby?" I asked.

He dropped to his knees in front of me, so I did the same. He was scaring me until he said, "Thank God. I never say anyone deserves what happens to them, but to hear this about her makes me happy. I feel bad about that but at the same time I don't. That was my son. They are seeking the death penalty."

Not being able to hide my satisfaction with what he said, I asked, "Really?"

"Yeah. Being that the crime was so heinous and led to Kendrick's death, they are giving it a try. I've never rejoiced in someone's pending death. I don't know how to feel about that."

I put my hands to his face. "Try not to analyze it right now. Your feelings are fresh. Kendrick's death is fresh. It hasn't even been a month yet. Give yourself time to process everything."

He nodded and I kissed his lips. "You're right, baby. Thank you."

I stood to my feet and grabbed his hand, watching his hair blow in the breeze. That shit was so sexy. Whenever I saw it, I wanted to hop his bones. Kenny was so fucking sexy, and the way he always looked at me only made my desire for him more intense. His laidback, loving personality just did it for me. Wrapping his arms around my waist, he kissed my lips and said, "I can't wait until tonight to dig up in that kitty cat."

He caught me off-guard with what he said, because I wasn't expecting him to go there just yet. However, I knew he was insatiable. He'd been that way since day one. I suppose it was a good thing that I was the same way. "I can't wait for you to dig deep, either. You know I always knew that I would never stop loving you, Kenny. We are in way too deep. You completely consumed me, and if I couldn't or wouldn't be with you, I knew in my heart that no one else would be able to get to where you had."

Pulling me closer and letting his hands slide down to my ass, he said, "Way too in deep, baby. I'm way too in deep."

I recognized the way he said it as Summer Walker's lyrics, and he was right. Pulling his face to mine, I kissed him deeply until I heard, "Daddy! Mommy! Come see me!"

Our kiss broke because of our laughter, then we held hands and stared at one another for a moment. "I guess we better go see what baby girl got going on, huh? It *is* her day."

"I guess we better or we will definitely hear about it," I responded.

Hand in hand, we made our way to see what baby girl was so excited about as I got a glimpse of Shylou hugging Cass. I hoped their attraction would go further than the surface, because they both deserved to be happy, especially Cass. When we got to the back, baby girl was riding her horse around barrels that Tiff had Ryder set up. I shook my head and knew that they were creating a monster. Karima reminded me so much of Tiffany, though, so if she followed in her footsteps, I wouldn't be mad about it at all.

❦

As I slid on the red, metallic-looking, floor length dress, I couldn't help but wonder why I was getting so dressed up. Kenny had left this box on the bed as I was showering. I knew he was taking me to dinner, but I never would have thought it would have been this fancy. The dress hugged my curves and it showed plenty of cleavage. The straps went around my arms and left my shoulders bare. It was a beautiful dress and I couldn't have done a better job at picking one myself.

I'd pinned my dreads up and curled the ones I left hanging in the front. Yesterday, when Kenny told me we'd be going to dinner, I rolled them on rods last night so they would be really curled like I wanted them. Once I was done, I headed downstairs to find my man already dressed. His hair was pulled up into a man bun and he wore some black dress pants, a black shirt, and a black suit jacket. Not a single hair was out of place and I could tell Jasper had killed his edges today, 'cause that shit was razor sharp.

He was standing there with a bouquet of roses, looking every bit of edible. "Damn, baby. You doing that dress a favor. You look sexy as hell."

"Kenny, you look amazing yourself, baby."

When I got to him, he pulled me in his embrace, running his nose along my jawline. He slid his hand down to my ass and said, "Mmm. You smell amazing. I almost wanna say fuck all this fancy shit and just stay home."

I giggled. Out of all his brothers, Kenny was more... I guess I could say citified. He rode horses and worked in the rice and hay fields and sometimes manned the grass farm, but he didn't mind getting dressed to impress. I loved that about him, because he was well-rounded. Jasper and Storm didn't get that way until they'd met their wives. And WJ, I still had yet to see him in a suit. I lifted my hand to his cheek and said, "It's your call, baby. I'll take all this shit off right here."

"Don't tempt me with a good time. But I wanna show you an amazing night out on the town. I know you like to get a lil snazzy every now and then."

"I do. This dress is perfect. Thank you, baby."

"Thank *you*, Keisha. You've been everything I been longing for.

The woman I fell so deeply in love with. Now, let's go. Our car is waiting, baby."

With that, he led me outside to see a beautiful Bentley waiting for us. "Oh, Kenny."

"Wait 'til you see the inside."

The outside was a silver-looking color, but when the driver opened the suicide doors, my lips parted. It was like a desert, red rock color. It was beautiful. Once I got in, instead of asking me to scoot over, Kenny went around to the other side. As tight as this dress was, it would have taken more of an effort to do so. When he got in, he asked, "So, what do you think?"

"I think this is a beautiful car, but not as amazing as the man I'm sitting next to."

"Oh yeah? Your man is more amazing than this three hundred fifty-thousand-dollar car?"

"Hell yeah. Easily."

I leaned over and kissed his lips as we took off, heading west on highway 90. If I had to guess, I would say we were going to Houston, but I would wait and see. During the ride, Kenny couldn't keep his hands off me and vice versa. My hands had to be on him in some way. Him sliding his fingertips over my shoulder was about to send me into orbit, though. When he replaced his fingertips with his lips, I closed my eyes and let a soft moan leave me. "Kenny, baby, you bringing me to the point of no return with all this affection."

"That's my intent, gorgeous. When tonight is all said and done, we'll be able to unleash all this pinned up desire on one another," he said close to my ear.

Shit if goosebumps didn't completely fill my flesh, then I wasn't living. The gushiness in the thong I was wearing was going to make me go to the nearest restroom and take it off as soon as we reached our destination. His lips kissed my neck, then he brought his hand to mine and held it the rest of the way.

As I thought, we were in Houston and had stopped at a restaurant called Steak 48. It looked exquisite and I couldn't wait to see what the food tasted like. Kenny got out the car and walked around to help me out as well. The passion in his eyes was somewhat overwhelming. While he was always passionate, it was something about it tonight that was threatening to take me down. My stomach had butterflies flapping all around inside it and a slight tremble went through my body. "What's wrong, baby?"

"Nothing is wrong. Everything about the way I'm feeling right now has me on a high I can't come down from. I feel so loved, adored, and cherished. I love you so much, Kenny."

"I love you, too, baby. With everything in me."

I could feel the tears brewing and I didn't understand why I was feeling so overwhelmed. When we walked inside, we were immediately escorted to our table. The setting was intimate, with two candles lit on the table covered with a white linen tablecloth. Kenny pulled out my chair, and once I sat, he pushed it in, then went around to his side of the table. After ordering us a bottle of wine, he said, "I just wanted tonight to be perfect and I feel it has been so far. What do you think?"

"It's been beyond perfect if there was such a thing."

We hadn't had much conversation, but it wasn't needed. Just his touch and soft spoken I love you's had been enough. Kenny had been everything my heart had missed from him. While the last five years of our marriage had gone down the drain, the first seven had been just like this.

Like a fairytale.

Like nothing else mattered.

Like it was us against the world.

After our wine had gotten to the table and the waiter had poured us each a glass, I took a sip as Kenny stared at me. He was starting to make me nervous, but I didn't say a word, only met his gaze and held it. He took a sip of his wine, then reached across the table to hold my hand. As he held it, he glanced down at my wedding ring. I'd been wearing it for a while now, at least for the past month. Since the day he hugged me and said he forgave me for everything and that he hoped I forgave him, too, I'd worn it every day.

When the waiter returned, we placed our orders and he swiftly walked away to put them in to the chef. Kenny again reached out for my hand and I gave it to him. Rubbing his thumb back and forth across the top of it, he said, "I was trying to wait until after we ate to do this, but I can't hold out any longer."

He slid my ring off my finger and my heart started to make its descent. Surely, he didn't bring me to this fancy-ass dinner to break things off with me. Standing from his chair, he put the ring in his pocket and pulled out a box. My eyes started to well up with tears when I realized he'd bought me another ring. It felt like I was hyperventilating. Walking over to me, he went to his knee and began, "Keisha, you're my world. I know I've told you before, but there's no other woman that completes me. God placed you in that grocery store parking lot that day, just for me."

Grabbing my hand, he kissed it and stared at it for a second, then looked back up at me. "To know that I fucked up and lost you for almost two years is hard to even think about. You left no stone unturned when it came to pleasing and loving me. I should have known something was wrong and took into consideration that you might have been scared to tell me. I don't plan to ever fuck up like that again. Had it not been for Kendrick, I know I would have self-destructed without you and my kids. When God took him, I realized that he was here to help me cope with my time away from you."

The tears were free-falling from my eyes. Listening to his beautiful words was so overwhelming. Kenny never had a problem pouring out his heart to me, but this time, it just felt like it meant more. Knowing that I'd fucked up, too, and that he still felt all that for me, took me down... fast. "Keisha, this time is gonna be different. I need to know that you trust me to not only please you in every aspect, but that you trust me not to take your heart through anything like that again."

"I trust you with everything in me, Kenny," I said as he swiped the tears away from my cheeks.

Glancing around the restaurant, I noticed we had a nice sized audience as he continued. "Well, there's nothing more for me to say, other than asking the big question. Keisha, will you do me the honor of being my wife again?"

"Before I answer that, I have to get down here with you." I got on my knees in that beautiful-ass gown, then looked up at him. Putting my hand to his cheek, I said, "You aren't the only one that messed up. I'm grateful that you chose to forgive me and want to make things work in our relationship. At first, I thought it was for the sake of our children, but I quickly realized that it was so much more. For you to want to marry me again, I know that your heart is pure and the love you have for me is immeasurable. Thank you for trusting me, even after I withheld things from you for years and made you seem like a heartless individual. You're an amazing man and I love you and will love you beyond my years here on earth. Yes, I will gladly be your wife again."

Kenny's eyes had never left mine as I spoke, and his eyes had watered as well. He refused to let a tear fall, though. When I finished, he slid the most beautiful ring I'd ever seen on my finger, then stood to his feet and helped me to mine, then kissed me passionately as onlookers applauded. When he pulled away, I looked down at the ring again. "Kenny, this ring is beautiful."

He smiled and said, "You should've seen the first one I picked out."

He chuckled, then took a sip of his wine. I could tell there was a story behind that, but I would hear it later. All I could think about now was spending the rest of my life as Mrs. Kendrall Dominic Henderson.

✼ 21 ✼

K enny

My knees were knocking as we stood outside the courtroom, waiting to enter for the trial. When the district attorney walked over to us, he shook my hand, then Keisha's. My entire family was standing behind us, even some of my sisters-in-law's parents were in attendance as well. Just our support system would fill the court-room. Cass had come from San Antonio and had driven in with Shylou. So, I supposed he'd finally gotten that issue handled. We hadn't talked much, because I was wrapped up in Keisha and stressing over this trial for the past week.

When the doors opened, we all filed in and just like I thought, we took up most of the seats. Everybody wanted to see her go down and suffer for what she did to Kendrick. My initial feelings about them trying to get the death penalty for her hadn't changed. I still wanted her to die for what she did to my son. That was probably something I would never forgive her for. Even though I felt God allowed everything to happen for a reason, I harbored so much hate in my heart for Tasha. It was at the point where I didn't give a damn about her or her life.

When we sat, all the fellas squeezed my shoulder as they passed by us to take their seats. My mama and daddy were seated directly behind us, along with Tiffany, Ryder, and my kids. Within minutes of us arriving and getting situated, guards led Tasha in. All chatter had ceased. It was so quiet, you could hear a rat piss on cotton. She looked like shit. Her face was somewhat swollen like somebody had fucked her up in there. I didn't feel the least bit of sensitivity for her. I was actually trembling from the anger coursing through me.

Keisha squeezed my hand, so I turned to look at her. Her eyes were warm and calm, so I held my gaze to hers for a while... until the jury entered the courtroom. I did my best not to even look at Tasha anymore as they sat. Half of them were black and most of them were women. I wasn't worried about that, though. They wouldn't sympathize with her ass. Not when it came to this. As I watched them, the judge entered the courtroom, so we all stood. Once he sat, we sat, and I was ready to get this show on the road and get it over with.

As the DA and court appointed defense attorney gave their opening arguments, I kept my line of vision on the jury or on me and Keisha's hands. But my mind stayed on Kendrick and the happy times I shared with him. Talks of him being murdered in cold blood was making me wanna go over there and choke Tasha to death. We'd be able to end her trial today, because I'd literally kill her. I gently rubbed Keisha's hand between mine as she wiped her tears with her other hand. Lifting my arm, I pulled her closer and rested it on her shoulder.

They'd warned me that I could be called to the witness stand to speak on Tasha's character if needed, but I hoped they didn't need me to. There was only one witness that was on the scene of the crime at some point and that was the neighbor that heard Kendrick scream-ing. However, when the picture of Kendrick appeared on the screen, I almost lost it. Turning my head, I coughed a couple of times, then lowered my head to my lap. I couldn't do this. The picture they showed the jury was to prove how he'd suffered. How that bleach had literally eaten him alive. Had I been paying attention to what was being said, I would have known they were about to show that picture. My kids' eyes were closed, and I was thankful they didn't have to see that.

Keisha had wrapped her arm around me as I said in a whisper, "My baby. I can't do this."

She rubbed my head and pulled me to her. "You can, baby. Justice has to be served for Kendrick, and I know you want to see it served. We are all here for you, baby," she whispered.

The DA had stopped for a moment to give me time to calm down, then he started again, telling the jury to look at how distraught I was and how loved Kendrick was by my side of the family. The courtroom was full of support for me, but no one was there for Tasha. The defense attorney obviously didn't do his research, because he'd tried to say that Tasha was overwhelmed with caring for a toddler. *How sway?* The DA jumped all over that, telling the jury that I provided all his care and that Tasha had only had him every other weekend for the past two months and before that not at all. They seemed to be in shock from that revelation.

The defense attorney was gonna get her charged a lot quicker and I wasn't mad about that. I didn't know why she just didn't take a plea agreement. There was no way she was going to get off for killing my son. I'd kill her first. The trial was short, simply because the defense attorney didn't know what the fuck he was doing. When I thought the jury was about to be dismissed to deliberate, the defense attorney called Tasha to the stand. I closed my eyes, because I couldn't stand to look at that bitch. "Can you state your name for the jury?"

"Tasha Demi Jackson."

Seemed like she'd told me her last name was something else, but I couldn't even remember that shit. I refused to open my eyes, though. "Can you tell the court what happened the evening that Kendrick passed away?"

"He had been crying all day, whining for his daddy and his mima, who I assumed was his sister, Karima. No matter what I did, he wasn't satisfied. He'd done well the night before, but that particular day, he was on my last nerve. I was tired from trying to calm him down all day. I snapped."

"Okay, Ms. Jackson, no further questions."

I had to open my eyes. That was the only questions he was gonna ask her? That was a bullshit ass job. The DA stood to question her. His first question was the one I was thinking the whole time she was talking. "If you felt overwhelmed, why didn't you call his dad? He was the custodial parent. He spent the most time with him. Why didn't you call him?"

She shrank a little in her seat. "I didn't want it to seem like I couldn't handle my own son."

"Ms. Jackson, remember you were sworn in and perjury is against the law. You wrote this note to his father about only wanting the child for the child support check. Why?"

"I wanted Kenny to hurt. He threw me out with the trash. After I told him I was pregnant, I expected him to step up to the plate and be with me... take care of me. But he didn't. Instead, he fought me for custody and took my baby from me. So, I took his baby from him!"

I opened my eyes and stood to my feet, ready to knock her ass off that witness stand. Jasper and Keisha stood on either side of me, trying to get me to sit. "You stupid bitch!" I yelled.

"Order! Mr. Henderson, if you can't control your outbursts, you're going to have to leave the courtroom."

I slowly sat in my seat as the tears left my eyes. Glancing over at the jury, I saw a couple of the women crying and most of them had disgusted expressions on their faces. I wanted to walk out the court-room to keep my sanity, but my heart needed to see this through. Seeing her found guilty was gonna be a part of my healing process. I was at peace, but knowing she was suffering from what she did would bring me joy. When the DA looked back at her, he said, "Did you not feel any remorse when you looked at what you did to that baby?"

"Not at first. After I had time to think about it, I regretted what I did, but it was too late at that point."

The DA frowned at her, then said, "No further questions."

When he sat, he turned to me and shook my hand. After that shit, they wouldn't need me on the witness stand. The judge announced that there would be closing arguments. I couldn't believe there wasn't really a defense. She could have used postpartum depression, tempo-rary insanity... shit. Any excuse was better than just wanting to hurt me. As they gave their closing arguments, I used that moment to calm myself down. I almost could have stayed home for this fiasco. Tasha was crazy out of her mind, and instead of finding pussy to dive into, I should have been trying to make things better with my wife.

The judge dismissed us for the jury to deliberate and when we got outside the courtroom, the DA stopped us. "I promise this won't take long. Don't go far. I give it thirty minutes tops. I can't believe she said the things she did on the stand. I applaud you, Mr. Henderson. I think I would have attacked her right there in the courtroom had that been my child." He shook my hand, then said, "See you all in a few minutes."

When he walked away, my family offered hugs and kisses. Seeing Legend, Red, Zay and Price there with their wives, made me feel even more loved. I was grateful for great friends. They were always there when I needed them. Before we could even get comfortable on the benches we'd sat on, they were calling us back in the courtroom. It had only been twenty minutes. Keisha grabbed my hand as we walked back inside, and I put my arm around her. This shit had been just as rough on her as it was on me. Once we sat, she said, "Baby, she's finally about to get what she deserves. Only a monster could do the things she did to Kendrick."

"I know, baby. I just want it to be over."

The jury walked in and I took a deep breath. If they didn't find her guilty, then all of them were just as crazy and demonic as Tasha's ass. When the judge came in, we stood, then sat when he did. "No need in prolonging this, since the jury didn't. Madam foreman have you reached a verdict?"

"We have your honor."

"What say you?"

"For the charge of torture, we find the defendant guilty."

Everyone clapped, then the foreman continued. "For the charge of first-degree murder, we find the defendant guilty."

Everyone clapped again and I hugged Keisha. She was gonna either get life in prison or the death penalty. My son died as a result of her torture. I finally looked at her as they handcuffed her and took her away. The scowl on my face was ever present, but when she smiled at me, I could have torn the fucking courtroom up. However, this was all done until the sentencing trial, which I didn't necessarily have to be at. Once we were dismissed by the judge and informed that sentencing would be in a week, we left the courtroom. It felt like a weight had been lifted off me, knowing there was no chance she would get away with murdering Kendrick. "I'm glad this is almost over, baby," I said to Keisha as we walked to the car.

"Me too, baby."

"So, have you thought about when you wanted to get married?" I asked as we got in the car.

"Yep. I told Tiffany to hook us up with something at the barn in two weeks. No point in waiting. I love you and I ain't going nowhere. Besides, this ain't our first rodeo.

"I suppose you're right. Let's do this."

"YOU LOOK NICE IN YOUR JEANS AND STETSON, KENNY, BUT I make this shit look sexy," Shylou said.

I rolled my eyes. "You sound like Storm. Plus, this prolly your first time in cowboy boots and a Stetson."

"It is, but that don't mean nothing. You see how Cass keep giving me the eye? I make this shit look good."

I shook my head slowly. Shylou was my best man, since Storm and Jasper were trying to battle each other for the position. They were both groomsmen along with KJ, Price and Ryder. Chrissy, Jenahra, Tiffany, Chasity, and Aspen were bridesmaids and Cass was Keisha's maid of honor. Karima was the flower girl and we chose not to do a ring bearer. Jasper's son would have turned our wedding out. My sisters and Keisha had done an amazing job decorating. It seemed this barn was used for everything and I couldn't help but to remember Kendrick and Karima's birthday parties, the numerous engagement parties, and the repast after Kendrick's funeral.

But today was a day of new beginnings and I couldn't wait to call Keisha my wife again. Although I was calling her my wife already, it would be official after today. When the music started, I knew we needed to get in our places. We'd rehearsed somewhat last night. It was almost impossible for my family to take anything seriously, especially the bottom three. Jasper, Tiffany, and Storm could ruin an entire celebration with their antics and Storm was the ringleader.

When the wedding party started to walk in, I couldn't stop the smile from spreading across my face, but when the song, "Nothing Even Matters" started to play, I knew my baby was about to walk in. It was what I told her all the time. The past was just that... the past, so leave it there. As long as we had each other and our family was good, nothing even mattered. When she appeared in her off the shoulder, cream-colored mermaid dress, I practically stopped breathing. She was so beautiful. The tulle that fell around her legs didn't hide a thing. The dress itself stopped about mid-thigh. Those chocolate legs were calling out to me and I couldn't wait to have them wrapped around my waist and neck tonight.

Seeing my dad walk her down the aisle was magical. Keisha never knew her biological dad and my dad had walked her down the aisle for our first wedding. He was more than honored to serve in that capacity once again. When she got to me, I couldn't help but pull her to me. The preacher cleared his throat, and Storm said, "Not yet, dummy."

Everyone chuckled quietly as the ceremony began. Keisha and I stared at one another the entire time and I knew I had gotten lost in her gaze until she began speaking. I realized she was saying her vows. "Kenny, throughout my entire adult life, you've been a constant in my life, even when I pretended I didn't want you to be. You're the most loving, forgiving person I've ever met. I've been smitten with you for close to twenty years. After dating for three years and we got married, I knew you were the man I would spend the rest of my life with. Despite our challenges and our almost two-year hiatus, God blessed us still. Being in love with you is the best feeling in the world and I'm grateful that you saw fit to make me your wife once again. I love you."

"Kenny, your vows."

"Well, I didn't prepare anything. I knew I could just speak from my heart about the limitless, agape love I have for you. My love for you never ceased. I couldn't even force myself to stop showing you how much I loved you. I probably only went two weeks where I didn't show you, if that long. Keisha you are my everything. There's no better feeling than to be standing here with you at this very moment, giving you my heart all over again, although it's been in your possession for a long time. As I told you before, you're the only woman I've ever loved and that I've ever wanted to love. Nothing else even matters. I love you Keisha."

After a brief memorial for Kendrick and a prayer, the preacher pronounced us husband and wife. The moment I'd been waiting for. I pulled Keisha to me and kissed her like there was no more tomorrow until Jasper said, "Dang, Kenny. Save some for the honeymoon."

I couldn't help but laugh against Keisha's lips and she did the same as everyone applauded. When we separated, she said, "Feeling the way I feel with you right now makes me believe the journey was worth it."

"No more secrets, no more worries about what the other will say, and no more falling into habits of infidelities. This is our new beginning and we've both been redeemed, forgiven, and blessed to accept one another once again. This is you and me, baby... forever."

EPILOGUE

K eisha
One year later...

"I HAVE HIM, KEISHA. HE'S A BEAUTIFUL BABY."

"Thanks, god-mommy Cass."

"All that unprotected sex got y'all having a baby old as hell."

"Shut up. I'm thirty-six, not fifty-six."

"Yeah, but that's late."

"Whatever."

Kenny and I had celebrated our new anniversary a few days ago and I was at Cass and Shylou's house to pick up our two-month-old, baby. He caught us both by surprise, but he was a welcomed blessing. We named him Kingsley Kendrick Henderson and called him King for short. While we weren't using protection and I wasn't on birth control, I still thought it would be nearly impossible to conceive. My cycles had slowed down to about five or six a year. God showed us differently. When he was born, Kenny nearly broke down at just how much he looked like Kendrick. But Kendrick looked like Kenny, so Kingsley looked like Kenny, too. But Kenny was so emotional about it. And I could understand that. "So how was Jamaica?"

"It was great. We had an amazing time. Thanks."

"Good."

"So, you and Shylou ain't get no ideas while y'all had my baby?"

"Girl, please say that in a lower voice. Ever since he found out that baby wasn't his and we got serious, he been on one. Just because I live here don't mean shit. I need more of a commitment before I go to having babies for his fine ass. He better put a ring on my shit."

I laughed as King stirred in Cass's arms. She handed him to me so I could get ready to go. Kenny was waiting in the car for me. We were just ready to get home. KJ and Karima were at Mom and Dad Henderson's house. They both wanted to stay near their horses so they could practice. KJ would be entering in his second rodeo in a couple of months. After Zay trained his horse a little better, Kenny was able to work with him on cutting, and KJ was amazing at it, maybe even better than Kenny. He'd placed third in the first rodeo. Tiffany had been working with Karima and she was doing great, too. She would probably be entering a rodeo soon as well.

Cass had begged us to keep Kingsley. Since they'd dropped us off to and picked us up from the airport, it wasn't an issue, although Mama Henderson was pissed about it. She wanted to keep Kingsley so bad. I had to inform her that there would be plenty of other opportunities for that. We'd gladly bring him right on over. He was a good baby, but Kenny and I took our alone time seriously these days. We seemed to always be doing things with the kids. Not only were they wanting to rodeo, but KJ played football and Karima was in dance. "I'm gonna bring his things to the car. Hold him for me and I'll be right back."

When I walked outside, I noticed Kenny was on the phone. He immediately got out of the car to help me with King's things. "Baby, everything okay? You look bothered."

He looked at me and said, "Tasha's execution date is coming

soon. They were calling to ask if we would be in attendance. While I'm not feeling sorry for her, I don't want to see the shit, either."

My mouth parted. I didn't see how anyone could watch someone get executed by choice. That shit would give me nightmares. "So, what did they say when you said you didn't want to be there?"

"Just that they understood. They would send notice once it had been done."

He shrugged his shoulders, then brought the things to the trunk. Once he came back, he pulled me to him. "We can't think about that right now. We had an amazing time on our trip and our lives have been beyond blessed. Let's keep that same energy and positivity."

"You right, baby."

"Oh, and Tiff called. Her and Milana will be by later."

"Okay. Let me go get our baby before Cass and Shylou disappear with him."

I kissed Kenny's lips, then headed back inside. Tiffany had a little girl name Milana. She was eight months old now and had a head full of hair. Tiff always came over to have me put her hair in different styles. So, I was sure that was the reason for this visit as well. Things were going great and I was blessed to be living this life with Kenny. He could have written me off that day in the condo in San Antonio and long before that, actually, but he didn't. We were made for each other and as he always said, we were in way too deep to move on.

THE END

AFTERWORD

From the Author

This story of redemption was tough to write, but Kenny wouldn't leave me alone until I told his story. His story tells you that you can't judge someone from what you hear from others or by what you think happened. Yes, he did wrong, but he wasn't that person. He wasn't the individual that didn't care. Knowing the circumstances that led to his wrongdoing can somewhat make you sympathize with him. He and Keisha both had issues that contributed to their demise, but true love prevailed even when most people would have been like hell naw, I'm done. They accepted their own flaws and the flaws within each other and chose to move on from it. So, I hope you enjoyed this story of love, pain, passion, and forgiveness.

There's also an amazing playlist on iTunes for this book under the same title that includes some great R&B tracks to tickle your fancy. Please keep up with me on Facebook (@authormonicawalters), Instagram (@authormonicawalters) and Twitter (@monlwalters). You can also visit my Amazon author page at www.amazon.com/author/

monica.walters to view my releases. Also, subscribe to my webpage for updates! www.authormonicawalters.com

For live discussions, giveaways and inside information on upcoming releases, join my Facebook group, Monica's Romantic Sweet Spot at https://bit.ly/2P2lo6X.

Upcoming book signing events:

Indie Love: June 27, 2020 in New Orleans, LA Register at www.indielovee.com

Atlanta Kickback: July 18, 2020 Free to the public at the Georgia International Convention Center

OTHER TITLES BY MONICA WALTERS

Love Like a Nightmare

Forbidden Fruit (An Erotic Novella)

Say He's the One

Only If You Let Me

On My Way to You (An Urban Romance)

8 Seconds to Love

Breaking Barriers to Your Heart

Any and Everything for Love

Savage Heart (A Crossover Novel with Shawty You for Me by T Key)

I'm In Love with a Savage (A Crossover Novel with Trade It All by T Key)

Don't Tell Me No (An Erotic Novella)

Training My Heart to Love You

To Say, I Love You: A Short Story Anthology with the Authors of BLP

Blindsided by Love

Drive Me to Ecstasy

Whatever It Takes: An Erotic Novella

Ignite My Soul

Never Enough (A Novella update of the Sweet Series Characters)

When You Touch Me

When's the Last Time?

Come and Get Me

Best You Ever Had

Deep As It Goes (A crossover novel with Perfect Timing by T. Key)

Behind Closed Doors Series

Be Careful What You Wish For

You Just Might Get It

Show Me You Still Want It

Sweet Series

Bitter Sweet

Sweet and Sour

Sweeter Than Before

Sweet Revenge

Sweet Surrender

Sweet Temptation

Sweet Misery

Sweet Exhale

Motives and Betrayal Series

Ulterior Motives

Ultimate Betrayal

Ultimatum: #lovemeorleaveme, Part 1

Ultimatum: #lovemeorleaveme, Part 2

Written Between the Pages Series

The Devil Goes to Church Too

The Book of Noah (A Crossover Novel with The Flow of Jah's Heart by T Key)

The Revelations of Ryan, Jr. (A Crossover Novel with All That Jazz by T Key)

CPSIA information can be obtained
at www.ICGtesting.com
Printed in the USA
LVHW111559051120
670844LV00003B/431